P9-ECL-756

Party girl Lucy Blayne has barely been out of the news ever since it was revealed that her husband cheated on her and embezzled from her business, stealing millions from her trust fund and from many of her prestigious clients at Prêt a Party. I understand she has quite rightly divorced him, but her business is struggling regardless.

Bravely, she's battling on, though, determined to transform her business back into the success it once was. Now her chief advisor is none other than incredibly trustworthy—and handsome—Marcus Canning, banker to the seriously rich and famous.

For years Marcus has been a confirmed bachelor, running a mile at the merest mention of the word *wedding*. But my sources, a variety of paparazzi journalists, have passed on to me that Marcus and Lucy have been caught *in flagrante* in a number of risqué locations! This couple is seriously hot for each other. Could it be that it's the great sex that has changed his mind?

An engagement announcement has been published in the Forthcoming Marriages section of every national newspaper. Marcus Canning is to wed Lucy in just a few weeks' time.

This will most definitely be the society wedding of the year....

ROMANCE

PENNY JORDAN has been writing for more than twenty years and has an outstanding record: over 150 novels published, including the phenomenally successful *A Perfect Family, To Love, Honor and Betray, The Perfect Sinner* and *Power Play,* which hit the *Sunday Times* and *New York Times* bestseller lists. Penny Jordan was born in Lancashire, England, and now lives in rural Cheshire.

Don't miss the next books in
Penny Jordan's hot new miniseries

Jet Set Wives

On sale August 2005:
Bedding His Virgin Mistress
#2481

On sale October 2005:
Expecting the Playboy's Heir
#2495

On sale December 2005:
Blackmailing the Society Bride
#2505

Available only from Harlequin Presents®! .

Penny Jordan

BLACKMAILING THE SOCIETY BRIDE

Jet Set Wives

HARLEQUIN®

TORONTO • NEW YORK • LONDON
AMSTERDAM • PARIS • SYDNEY • HAMBURG
STOCKHOLM • ATHENS • TOKYO • MILAN • MADRID
PRAGUE • WARSAW • BUDAPEST • AUCKLAND

ISBN 0-373-12505-4

BLACKMAILING THE SOCIETY BRIDE

First North American Publication 2005.

Copyright © 2005 by Penny Jordan.

www.eHarlequin.com

Printed in U.S.A.

CHAPTER ONE

'SO WHAT you're saying is that my ex-husband has damaged my business so badly that it and I are both virtually bankrupt?'

Lucy stared at her solicitor. A deepening sense of sickening shock and fear was gripping her, a feeling that the situation she was involved in was so frightening and unbearable that it could not possibly be real.

But it was real. She was here, seated in front of Mr McVicar, while he told her that her ex-husband had so badly damaged the reputation and financial status of the event organisation company she had set up with such enthusiasm and delight prior to their marriage that it was no longer viable.

Nick had cheated her sexually and financially all through their brief marriage...but then, hadn't she done some cheating herself? A guilty conscience wasn't going to help her now, Lucy warned herself, as she struggled with the massive weight of the problems she now faced.

'I've got some commissions for events for the rest of this year,' she told the solicitor, crossing her fingers behind her back and hoping that he wouldn't ask her how many, since in reality there were so few. 'Perhaps, in view of that, the bank...?'

Her solicitor shook his head. He liked his pretty young client, and felt very sorry for her, but in his opinion her nature was too gentle for the unforgiving world of business.

'I'm sorry, my dear,' he told her. 'As you've already

said yourself, several potential clients have cancelled their events and asked for their deposits back already, and I'm afraid... Well, let's just say we live in a harsh world, where confidence is something no one can put a price on.'

'And because of what Nick has done no one will have any confidence in Prêt a Party any more—is that what you mean?' Lucy asked him bitterly. 'Even though Nick is no longer a part of the business, or my life, and I was the one who started it up in the first place?'

The solicitor's sympathetic look was all the answer she needed.

'I dare say I shouldn't blame clients for backing out. After all, I suppose in their eyes if I was stupid enough to marry Nick then I can't have much credibility,' Lucy said with bitter humour. That was certainly what Marcus believed. She knew that well enough.

Marcus. If there was one person she would like to somehow magically remove from her life and her memories for ever, that person wasn't Nick, but Marcus.

'Is there nothing I can do to save the business?' She appealed to her solicitor.

'If you could find a new partner—someone of probity and known financial stature, whom people respect and trust, and who is willing to inject enough capital to settle all Prêt a Party's outstanding obligations...'

'But I intend to pay those off *myself*. I still have money in my trust fund,' Lucy interrupted fiercely.

'Yes, of course. I realise that. But I'm afraid that clearing Prêt a Party's debts, whilst a very honourable thing to do, will not revive client confidence in you, Lucy. Regrettably, the actions of your ex-husband have damaged the reputation of the business virtually beyond repair, and the fact that both your partners have left Prêt a Party—'

'But that's because they both got married and have other

responsibilities now, that's all. Not because of anything else! Carly's pregnant and has her son to look after, as well as working alongside Ricardo with the orphanages he has set up, and Julia has a new baby to look after—plus she's involved in the Foundation—'

'Of course.' Her solicitor soothed her sympathetically. 'I know all this, Lucy, but unfortunately the eyes of the outer and greater world—the world from which you hope to attract new business—do not see it. I really am sorry, my dear.' He paused. 'Have you thought of approaching Marcus? He—'

'No! Never! And I absolutely and totally forbid you to say anything about any of this to him, Mr McVicar.' Lucy spoke fiercely, standing up so abruptly that she almost knocked over her chair. Panic and misery gripped her by the throat as powerfully as though it were Marcus himself closing his fingers around it. How he would love this. How he would love telling her that he had warned her all along that this would happen. How he would look down that aristocratic nose of his with those ice-cold eyes while he ticked off a list of all that she had done wrong, all the ways in which she had failed.

Sometimes, in the eyes of her family and Marcus, Lucy felt as though she had spent the whole of her life failing. For a start she had been a girl and not a boy, a daughter and not a son—a daughter to be married off and not a son to be an heir. And, even though her parents had gone on to have a son, Lucy had somehow always felt she had let them down by being born first, and the wrong sex. Not that her parents had ever said that she was a disappointment to them, but Lucy had been born with a sensitive kind of nature and did not need to be told what people felt. She had sensed her parents' disappointment—just as in later years she had recognised Marcus's impatient irritation with her.

Not that anyone ever needed to *guess* what Marcus thought or felt. She had never known anyone more capable of or uncompromising about saying exactly what he thought and felt. And he had made it plain from the first moment he had confronted Lucy across the large desk in his London office that he did not approve of the fact that her late great-uncle had left her such a large sum of money.

'I suppose that's why you agreed to be my trustee, is it?' Lucy had accused him. 'Because you don't approve of me having the money and you want to make life as difficult for me as possible!'

'That kind of remark merely confirms my concern about your late great-uncle's mental state when he made his will,' had been Marcus's caustic response.

'I suppose you were hoping he would leave his money to you?' Lucy had shot back.

In response, Marcus had given her a look that had made her face burn, and made her feel as though she wanted to crawl into a corner.

'Don't be so bloody infantile,' he had told her coldly.

Of course she hadn't realised then that Marcus had millions, if not billions of his own, tucked away in the vaults of his family's merchant bank, of which he was the CEO.

Mr McVicar watched her sympathetically. He knew perfectly well of the tension and ill feeling that existed between his client and the formidably wealthy banker her late great-uncle had appointed as trustee for the money he had left her.

That money had nearly all gone now—swallowed up by the greed and fraudulent actions of Lucy's ex-husband and the failure of her once-successful small business.

But in his view there was still no one better placed to

help her in her present difficult situation than Marcus, whose business savvy was both awesome and legendary. Mr McVicar himself had urged her not to agree to her bank's request that she secure Prêt a Party's finances by pledging her inheritance, but she had refused to listen to him. Morally Lucy was beyond reproach, but unfortunately she had been too gullible for her own good, and she was paying the price for that now.

He returned to the problem at hand. 'If you could attract a wealthy business partner who would be prepared to put money into the business, then—'

'Actually, that's exactly what I've been doing.'

As soon as the words had left her mouth Lucy wondered what on earth she was doing. Was it Mr McVicar's reference to Marcus that had prompted her into lying to him and creating a fictional potential backer? Lucy closed her eyes in helpless acknowledgement of her own vulnerability. Somehow just hearing Marcus's name was enough to goad her into a fury of defensiveness.

Mr McVicar looked both relieved and surprised.

'Well, that is really excellent news, Lucy. It puts a different complexion on matters entirely,' he told her enthusiastically, looking so pleased that her guilt increased uncomfortably. 'The very best outcome one could have hoped for, in fact. But obviously it is something we shall need to discuss. I think we should set up a meeting with your proposed partner and his or her legal advisers just as soon as we can. Oh, and of course we must let your bank know what is in the wind. I am sure that they will be inclined to be far more flexible once they know that fresh capital will be injected into Prêt a Party. I also think it would be a good idea to go public, even perhaps take a half-page announcement in those papers most frequently read by your clients stating once again that your ex-husband now has no access to or involvement with any aspect of Prêt a Party's business, and that moreover you now have a new partner. That should do a tremendous amount to offset the upsetting effect Nick's fraudulent behaviour has had on the business.'

Lucy felt as though she were trapped in ever-deepening mud of a particularly sticky and clinging consistency. Why on earth had she let the thought of Marcus's disapproval propel her into such stupidity? What on earth had she done? How could she admit now to Mr McVicar that she had lied—and why?

'Er, I can't tell you who he is at the moment, Mr McVicar,' Lucy began uncomfortably. 'It's all very much a secret. Negotiations are...um...well, you know how it is...'

'Of course. But I must urge you to remember, Lucy, that time is very much of the essence here.'

Nodding her head, Lucy made her escape as quickly as she could. How could she have lied like that? It went against everything she believed in. Now she felt sickeningly guilty and ashamed of herself, and she had to blink away her self-pitying tears as she stood outside her solicitor's Mayfair office in the bright autumn sunshine.

What on earth was she going to do? It would take a miracle to save her now. Automatically, she turned the corner and hurried into Bond Street, not bothering to glance into the windows of the expensive shops lining the street. Designer label clothes were not really her thing. She liked vintage clothes, salvaged from street markets and family attics. Their fabrics were so lush, the feel of them against her skin something she treasured and loved: real silk and satin cashmere; sturdy wool; cool cotton and linen. Man-made fibres might be more practical for modern-day city living, but in many ways she was an old-fashioned girl who craved a return to a quieter, more gentle way of life.

The truth was that secretly she would have loved nothing more than to marry and produce a large brood of much-loved children whom she and her husband would raise in an equally large and loved country house. She envied her two best friends their happy marriages and new young families more than they or anyone else knew—after all, she had her pride, just like anyone else. It was that pride that had led her into setting up Prêt a Party in the first place. The very same pride that had just led her into telling that stupid, stupid lie, she reminded herself miserably.

The magazines on a nearby newsstand caught her eye, and she stopped to study them. To the forefront, as always, was *A-List Life*. Lucy started to smile.

Its eccentric owner and editor Dorland Chesterfield had been such a good friend to her, using Prêt a Party to organise several of the events he had hosted—events attended by the world's top celebrities. She might even have considered turning to *him* for help to get her out of the mess Nick had left her in were it not for the fact that she knew if there was anything guaranteed to overwhelm his genuine kind-heartedness it was his love of passing on gossip. The last thing she needed right now was to have the story of her downfall spread over the pages of *A-List Life*.

Of course both her friends—now ex-partners in Prêt a Party—had extremely wealthy husbands, and both of them had in turn come to see her and gently offered financial help, but Lucy could not accept it. For one thing there was that wretched pride of hers, and for another it was not just money she needed, but someone to work in the business with her. Being given money to clear Prêt a Party's debts was a kind gesture, but she wanted—*needed*, in fact—to prove that she was not the silly fool everyone obviously thought her, and that she could make a success of her business.

Yes, marrying Nick had been a mistake, and, yes, she had—as Marcus had unmercifully pointed out to her—rushed into the marriage, but she'd had her own reasons for doing that. Reasons she could never, ever allow Marcus to discover.

She picked up a copy of *A-List Life* and handed over some coins, giving a reciprocal smile to the newsstand vendor before turning to cross the road. The sunlight glinting on her shoulder-length naturally blonde hair caused the driver of a large, highly polished, diplomat-plated Mercedes to slow down and study her appreciatively.

As she regained the pavement Lucy flipped open the magazine and quickly checked the contents—more out of habit than anything else. It was over three months now since Prêt a Party had managed a large event of any kind, never mind one glitzy enough to merit page-space in Dorland's magazine, but to her astonishment she suddenly saw Prêt a Party's name beneath the words: *A-List Life*'s Favourite Party of All Time.'

Bemused, she turned the pages, her eyes widening as she recognised the photographs covering the entire mid-section of the magazine. They were from the huge summer party Prêt a Party had organised for *A-List Life* the previous year.

Tears stung her eyes. It was so typical of Dorland to do something so generous—and it *was* generous of him to republish those photographs, even if at the same time it was also a way of blowing his own trumpet.

Although at the time she had refused to admit it to anyone, she had known then that her marriage had been a mistake, and she had known, too, that Nick was being unfaithful. She had known that Nick was cheating on her, yes, but she had not known that he was also defrauding her business and her customers—even if her two best friends Carly and Julia *had* suspected what was happening.

Out of concern for her they had kept their suspicions to themselves. Not so Marcus. Lucy knew that she would never be able to forget the searing humiliation of having to stand in front of Marcus whilst he listed with cold fury the fraudulent activities Nick had been engaged in whilst in charge of finances in Prêt a Party.

'Why the hell did you marry him in the first place?' he had demanded savagely, before adding, 'No, don't bother to tell me. I already know the answer. Did it never occur to you that you could have sex with him *without* marrying him?'

Lucy's face burned hotly now, just remembering how Marcus had looked at her.

'Perhaps I wanted more than sex,' she had countered. She *had* wanted more, certainly, but she had not received it. But then, neither had she given Nick more. And as for the sex... Her face burned again, but for a different reason.

The Nick who had spoken so urgently and flatteringly of his desire for her before their marriage had very quickly turned into a Nick who derided and taunted her for her lack of sexual expertise and desirability after it. And who could blame him? The effort of maintaining the fantasy of hot, urgent longing for him with which she had thrown herself into their relationship had proved too much for her to sustain once they were married. Nick had taunted her for her sexual inexperience, claiming that she was frigid and she turned him off, and she had been in too much torment, compounded by her guilt and self-loathing, to protest.

'More than sex? Really? And you actually thought you

would get more from someone like him?' he had demanded sarcastically.

'It's all very well for you to stand there and—and criticise me,' Lucy had told him wildly. 'But I don't see that *you* are exactly having any success with a long-term relationship!'

'Maybe that's because I haven't chosen to commit to one. I can certainly assure you that when I do my commitment to it and my conviction about it will be properly thought out and permanent. My decision won't be made off the back of imagining myself in love following an alfresco holiday shag.'

Lucy's hands tightened into impotent fists now, just remembering those contemptuous words, and the manner in which they had been delivered, with Marcus looking at her with that arrogant, obnoxious, *Marcus* look of his.

She had tried to defend herself, of course. 'That was not—I was not—' she had begun, but typically Marcus had refused to allow her to continue. 'Oh, come off it, Lucy,' he'd said harshly, 'we all know what happened. After all, the photographs were plastered all over the celebrity gossip rags. You, minus bikini top, draped all over Blayne, saying that you were up for a good time and looking for everything that went with that.'

'Goodness,' she had retaliated, in a brittle voice, 'you've actually remembered the caption word for word. Did you have to practise repeating it for very long to do that, Marcus?'

Of course she had regretted the idiotic quote recorded in the magazine. But when you were jet lagged, and you'd packed in such a rush that you'd omitted to pack matching bikini tops and bottoms, and you got caught out and papped by some prowling paparazzi with nothing better to do and no one better to photograph, you naturally did your best to make a joke of your plight—especially when those same paparazzi could sometimes be so important to the success of your business.

Not all celebrities, no matter what they might choose to say in public, genuinely wanted to avoid those camera lenses. Many actively sought out the events and parties where they would be spotted and photographed. Thus, Lucy had felt she could not afford to offend the guy who had snapped her, no matter what her own personal feelings.

If he'd seen her twenty-four hours later, then the photograph he would have taken would have been a very different one. Then, after a decent night's sleep and with the loan of a bikini from Jules, she would probably have been in control enough to tell him truthfully that she was simply taking a much-needed holiday from the mounting stress of running a successful business.

Unfortunately the photographer had taken it into his head that her life was far more interesting than it actually was, and from then on neither he nor his camera had been very far from her side.

Nick had revelled in the attention. At the time she had taken that as a sign that, unlike the other men she had dated, he would be able to cope with her work and its effect on their personal life. She hadn't realised that for Nick everything had its price—including photographs of them together, if not actually having sex in a variety of exotic locations then as close to it as was possible, given that she was wearing bikini bottoms and he was wearing swimming shorts.

She had had no idea that she was being set up with a view to them being taken until it was too late and they had been published. And by then she and Nick were married—

Naturally in public she'd had to shrug off her real feelings and pretend that she welcomed her new image as a randy, anything-goes, up-for-it and eager for sex party girl, only too delighted to let the whole world see how much she wanted her new husband. Even if by then that same new husband had been privately calling her frigid and useless in bed, and spending more nights out of their marriage bed than he was spending in it with her.

She looked at her watch a little bit anxiously. She had spent rather longer with her solicitor than she had expected, and she was due to put in an appearance at her great-aunt Alice's ninetieth birthday party this afternoon.

Great-Aunt Alice lived in Knightsbridge, in a huge old-fashioned apartment that was always freezing cold because, despite her wealth, she refused to have the central heating on.

No one in the family ever wanted to visit her in winter, and even in summer the wise visited equipped with extra layers in the form of cardigans, pashminas and the like, to ward off the icy blasts which Great-Aunt Alice insisted were necessary for good health and were the reason she was still hale and hearty at ninety.

'Balls,' Lucy's younger cousin Johnny had always claimed. 'The reason she's still alive is because she's too bloody mean to die. God knows, I could do with my share of her millions.'

'What makes you think you'll get a share?' Lucy's brother Piers had asked wryly.

'I'm bound to,' Johnny had replied smugly. 'I'm her favourite.'

'Yah? Well, you certainly work hard enough at it,' Piers had mocked him.

Nineteen-year-old Johnny, with his slightly louche lifestyle, permanent lack of money and winning ways, had a reputation within the family of being someone who was constantly wheeling and dealing. Lucy suspected that

Marcus probably disapproved of Johnny almost as much as he did her.

Marcus! But *she* didn't disapprove of *him*, did she? And that was the cause of, if not all, then surely most of the problems in her life. It had, after all, been to escape from loving Marcus and the knowledge that that love would never be returned that she had thrown herself into Nick's arms. And it was because she still loved Marcus now, despite all her attempts to stop doing so, that she treated him with hostility and resentment. That was her shield, her only protection against the potential humiliation of Marcus—or anyone else—ever discovering how she felt about him.

CHAPTER TWO

'GOODNESS. It's actually *warm* in here!' Lucy removed the cashmere wrap she had pulled on over her delicate silk chiffon dress the moment she walked into Great-Aunt Alice's hallway.

'Yes, I bribed Johnson to put the heat on.' Her brother Piers grinned.

'You might have told me that before,' Lucy grumbled affectionately, as she fanned herself with her hand to cool down her flushed face. 'How warm did you tell him to make it? It's like a sauna in here. The flowers I've bought Great-Aunt Alice will have wilted before she gets them.'

'Never mind your flowers—what about my chocolates?' Piers told her ruefully.

'Piers thought Johnson was probably still working in Fahrenheit,' Lucy's father chipped in. 'So he told him to set the temperature gauge at sixty-eight. None of us realised what had happened until Johnson came back and said that the gauge only went to forty.'

Lucy joined in the good-natured laughter at her brother's expense, and then suddenly froze as the door opened and Marcus walked in.

Was it her imagination or was there really a small, sharp silence—as though not just she but everyone else was aware of just how formidable and commanding Marcus was?

It wasn't only that he was tall—just nicely over six foot—or even that he was sexily broad-shouldered and taut-muscled. It wasn't even that combination of thick dark hair and striking ice-grey eyes which could sometimes burn almost green.

So what was it about him that made not just her own sex but men as well turn and look towards him? Turn and look up to him, Lucy amended.

Could it have something to do with the fact that he ran the merchant bank which had been in his family for so many generations? Because of that he was in a position of great trust, responsible not just for the present and future of his clients, but in many cases for the secrets of their ancestors as well.

But even if one took away all of that—even if he had walked in as a stranger off the street—women would still have turned their heads to look at him and would have gone on looking, Lucy acknowledged. Because Marcus was sexy. In fact, Marcus was *very* sexy. Her heart attempted to do a high dive inside her chest, then realised it was attempting the impossible and ended up crashing sickeningly to its floor. She gulped at the glass of champagne Piers had handed to her as much for something to do—some reason not to have to look at Marcus—as for Dutch courage.

He was wearing one of his customary hand-made plain dark suits, a typical banker's white shirt with a blue stripe, and a red tie.

She took another gulp of her champagne.

'Want another?' Piers asked her.

Lucy shook her head. She wasn't much of a drinker anyway, and her work meant that it was essential she kept a clear head in social situations, so she had quickly learned to simply take a small sip from her glass and then abandon it discreetly somewhere. The up side of this was that she always had a clear head, but the down side was that her body was simply not up to dealing with anything more than one small glass of anything alcoholic. But right now the numbing effect of a couple of glasses of champagne was probably just what she needed to help her cope with Marcus's presence, intimidatingly up close, if not exactly as personal as her foolish heart craved.

'Oh, good. Marcus has made it after all,' Lucy heard her mother exclaiming to Lucy's great-uncle in a pleased voice. 'Charles, do go over and ask him to join us.'

'Goodness, it *is* hot,' Lucy said wildly. 'I think I'd better go and get these poor flowers into some water.'

Her heart was thumping its familiar message to her as she made her escape, champagne glass in hand, heading for the rambling patchwork of corridors and small rooms to the rear of the huge apartment which her great-aunt still referred to as the servants' quarters.

How on earth did Johnson and Mrs Johnson, aided only by a daily, manage to cope with looking after somewhere this size? Lucy wondered sympathetically as she hurried down one of the corridors and into the 'flower room'. A row of vases had already been assembled on the worktop, ready filled with water, and Lucy unwrapped her own offering and busied herself placing the flowers stem by stem into water.

Was she really so afraid of seeing Marcus? Her hands trembled. Did she really need to ask herself that question? How old was she? Twenty-nine. And how long had it been since she had come down from university and looked at Marcus across the width of his desk and known...?

Tears suddenly blurred her vision.

Oh, yes, she had known then, immediately, that she had fallen in love with him, but she had known with equal immediacy that he did not return her feelings—that in fact, so far as he was concerned, her presence in his life was an inconvenience and an irritation he would far rather have been without.

She had been young enough then to dream her foolish dreams regardless, to fantasise about things changing, about walking into Marcus's office one day and having Marcus look at her as though he wanted to drag her clothes off and possess her right there and then. She had whiled away many an irascible lecture from Marcus by allowing herself the pleasure of imagining him standing up and coming towards her, taking hold of her and putting his desk, or sometimes his chair, more often than not both of them, to the kind of erotic use for which they had definitely not been designed.

But the reality was, of course, that she was the one who wanted to tear *his* clothes off. And then one day she had looked at him and seen the way he was looking at her. And she had known that her foolish erotic fantasies and her even more foolish romantic daydreams were just that. Marcus did not either want or love her, and he was never going to do so. That was when she had decided that she needed to find someone else—because if she didn't one day her feelings were going to get too much for her and she was going to totally humiliate herself by declaring them to Marcus.

A husband and then hopefully a family of her own would stop her from doing that, surely? she'd thought. But she hadn't even managed to get *that* right, had she? Her marriage had been a disaster—privately and publicly. Very publicly.

She wasn't the kind of person who wanted to be alone. She loved children, and had known from a young age that she wanted her own. Although she loved them both dearly, sometimes she felt wretchedly envious of the love and happiness her two best friends had found with their husbands.

And one day she knew Marcus would marry—and when he did... A shudder of vicious pain savaged her emotions.

When he did, she made herself continue, she hoped to be protected from what she knew she would feel by the contentment and love she had found with another man and her family. How foolishly and dangerously she had deluded herself.

She couldn't stay here in the flower room for ever, Lucy realised, and with any luck Marcus might actually have already left by now. Giving her flowers a final tweak, she turned to leave.

As soon as she opened the door into the drawing room the first person she saw was her cousin Johnny, who grabbed her arm and announced eagerly, 'Great—I've been looking for you. More champagne?' Without waiting for her to respond, he took a glass from a passing waiter and handed it to her.

'Must say the old girl isn't stinting with the champers. It must be costing her a pretty penny to put this do on. Champers...waiters. Did you organise it?'

'Yes,' Lucy said ruefully, remembering the hard bargain her great-aunt had driven over costs, and how in the end she had given in and suggested she give Great-Aunt Alice the business cost as her birthday present, provided her great-aunt supplied the champagne, the *hors d'oeuvres* and the waiters' wages. Which probably explained the lack of any food, Lucy decided.

She tried not to look at Marcus, who was standing the full width of the room away from her but facing towards her, and watching her, she could see, with a very grim look tightening his mouth. She took a quick, nervous, sustaining sip of her champagne, and then another. She couldn't bear to think about what would happen if Marcus ever got to hear about that idiotic lie she had told Mr

McVicar. In the absence of a miracle, she was going have to dispose of her supposed investor as speedily as she had invented him.

'Actually, Luce, there's something I need to discuss with you.'

'What?' Somehow or other Lucy managed to drag her attention away from Marcus.

'I need to talk to you,' Johnny repeated patiently.

'You do?' Immediately Lucy was alert to her own prospective danger. 'Johnny, if it's a loan you're after,' she began warningly, 'I haven't forgotten that you still owe me fifty pounds from last time. Even if you have.'

'It isn't anything like that,' Johnny assured her earnestly. 'Fact is, sweet cos, it just so happens that a business acquaintance of mine has asked me if I would introduce you to him.'

'He has?' Lucy said cautiously.

'Mmm. Have another glass of champagne,' he added encouragingly, removing Lucy's half-empty glass before she could refuse or protest and summoning the still-circulating waiter so that he could hand her a fresh glass.

On the other side of the room Marcus's unwavering focus on her had hardened into a grim-mouthed coldness that caused Lucy's hand to tremble so much she almost spilt her champagne.

'If he's thinking of commissioning Prêt a Party to do an event for him...' she began, trying to move round so that she couldn't see Marcus, and failing as he moved too.

'No, what he's got in mind is making an investment in Prêt a Party.'

'What?' Now she did spill a few drops of her champagne, before managing to take a steadying gulp of it.

'Oh, yes. He's a bit of an entrepreneur. He's made absolutely stacks of money from this turnkey business he owns. You know the kind of thing...' Johnny enlarged. 'He employs cleaners, cooks, someone to wait in for the gas man, someone to collect your cleaning—all that kind of stuff—for these rich City types who can't afford the time to do it themselves. He saw the spread in *A-List Life*, and heard that you're my cousin, and he said that Prêt a Party is exactly the kind of investment he's looking for. So I said I was seeing you today and that I'd sound you out.'

'Johnny...' Her head was spinning, and it didn't occur to her to connect that with her unfamiliar consumption of champagne.

'Why don't you let him talk to you and tell you what he's got in mind himself? I could give him your office phone number...'

When she had reflected that she needed a miracle she'd never imagined she would get one—and certainly not one of this potential magnitude. She felt positively light-headed with relief, almost dizzy.

'Well, yes—okay, Johnny,' she agreed gratefully.

'Great.' Johnny looked at his watch, announcing, 'Lord, is that the time? I've got to go. His name's Andrew Walker, by the way.'

She hadn't finished her champagne, but she put her glass on the tray as the waiter went past, absent-mindedly picking up a fresh glass and wincing slightly as she did so. She knew she shouldn't have worn these high heels. Shoes were Julia's thing, not hers, and she had only been persuaded into buying the strappy sandals with their far too high thin heels because they were the perfect shade of cornflower-blue to wear with one of her favourite dresses.

Unfortunately, though, they were not parquet-floor-friendly—especially when that floor had been polished in the old-fashioned way and was as slippery as an ice rink.

She looked round the room, but she couldn't see either

her parents or her brother, and she was just wondering if she could make her own escape when suddenly Marcus was standing in front of her, announcing grimly, 'Don't you think you've had enough?'

Enough of what? Lucy wanted to ask him. *Enough of loving you? Enough of wanting you and aching for you? Enough of dreaming of you whilst the man I married because I couldn't have you slept in bed beside me? Enough of knowing that you are never ever going to love me?* Oh, yes, she'd had enough of that.

'Actually, Marcus, no—I don't.' The familiar pain was back, and it was intensifying with every second she had to spend in his company. It seared her and drove her, maddening her with its agonising ache so that she barely knew what she was saying.

Marcus was looking at her with familiar contempt and irritation. Lucy gasped in dismay as someone standing behind her accidentally bumped into her. The combined vertiginous effects of stilettos and Marcus-induced heartache was definitely not good for one's balance, Lucy thought miserably, as Marcus gripped her arm firmly to steady her.

'Just how much champagne have you had?' Marcus demanded grimly.

'Not enough,' Lucy answered, with a flippancy she didn't feel.

Marcus was looking at her with a blend of irritation and impatience. 'You can hardly stand,' he told her critically.

'So what?' Lucy tossed her head. She was defying Marcus—baiting him, in fact! What on earth was happening to her? She was winding him up, and pushing her luck as she did so. She knew that, but somehow she couldn't help herself. Somehow she needed to see that look of angry irritation mixed with contempt in his eyes just to remind herself of the futility of dreaming impossible dreams.

'Actually, I rather think I'd like some more champagne. I'm celebrating, you see,' she heard herself telling him, uncharacteristically and recklessly emptying her glass before he could remove it and then looking round for the waiter with what she didn't realise was champagne-induced vagueness. Her lips did feel slightly numb, it was true, but then so did her toes, and they hadn't had any contact whatsoever with the champagne, had they?

'Celebrating what?' Marcus demanded tersely, his hold on her arm tightening.

'My miracle,' Lucy responded, forming the words very carefully.

She might have imagined it, but she thought Marcus actually swore softly. 'The only miracle here is that you're still standing,' he muttered.

The waiter was almost level with her. She reached out to pick up a full glass of champagne from the tray he was carrying, but Marcus got there before she could lift the glass, the fingers of his free hand closing hard on her own.

'Leave it where it is, Lucy,' he commanded her calmly.

'I'm thirsty,' Lucy protested. Thirsty for the nectar of his kiss, thirsty for the feel of his mouth on her own, on her skin, *everywhere*, whilst she drank in the taste of him. She looked at his hand, at his long, strong fingers curled around her own. She wanted to put her other hand on top of it, so that she could touch him. She wanted to lift his hand to her mouth so that she could breathe in the scent of his skin as she explored it with her lips and with her tongue. Longing burned through her, leaping from nerve-ending to nerve-ending until she was filled with it, possessed by it...

'I think it's time we left.' The cool hardness of Marcus's voice chilled her overheated thoughts.

'We?' she queried warily.

'Yes. *We*. I was just about to leave—and, unless you want the remainder of your great-aunt's guests to witness the unedifying sight of you sprawled on her parquet floor, I rather think you would be wise to leave with me. In fact, I am going to insist on it.'

'You're my trustee, Marcus, not my guardian or my keeper.'

'Right now, I'm a man very close to the edge of his patience. And besides, I need to talk you about Prêt a Party.'

Lucy stiffened defensively.

'If you're going to lecture me about Nick again—' she began, but Marcus simply ignored her and continued as though she hadn't interrupted him.

'You may remember me mentioning some time ago that my sister Beatrice wants to plan a surprise party for her husband's fiftieth birthday?'

'Yes,' Lucy agreed. Beatrice was Marcus's elder sister, and her husband George was something very important in the mysterious highest echelons of the civil service.

'I have to go and see Beatrice later this week, and she suggested that I should take you along with me so that she can discuss her party with you. I thought you might want to check your diary before we fix on a date.'

Lucy exhaled weakly. She was grateful to be given any business right now—even if it meant having to spend time with Marcus in order to obtain it.

'I've got a fairly free week,' she responded, as nonchalantly as she could. The truth was that she had a wholly free week; in fact the only event she had coming up in the whole of the next month was a launch bash for a sports-wear manufacturer.

Somehow or other they had actually reached the door to the hallway, where her great-aunt was already saying

goodbye to some of her other guests, and it was obvious
that Marcus had every intention of hauling her through it.
If she dug in her heels, would he literally drag her across
the parquet?

'You're walking too fast,' she told him breathlessly, and
then gave a small startled 'oof' of exhaled breath as he
stopped so suddenly that she cannoned straight into him.

She was standing body to body with Marcus, and he had
one hand on her arm whilst his other was pressed into the
small of her back. She could smell the faint lemony scent
of his cologne, mixed with warm man scent. Suddenly the
back of her throat prickled treacherously with tears. How
many hours had she wasted after she had first smelled it
on him haunting the men's toiletries departments of upmarket stores? Sniffing and testing and searching, hoping
that she might recognise it and find out just what it was
he wore, so that she could buy some and put a little on
her pillows, so that she could wear it herself if necessary—
anything just to be able to feel closer to him. But she had
never discovered what it was.

Body to body with Marcus. If only by some miracle he
would draw her closer now, and bend his head and cover
her mouth with his—if only, if only...

'Marcus, dear boy—so good of you to come. And
Lucy...'

Lucy could feel her face burning as Marcus stepped
back from her but still continued to hold on to her arm.

The almost flirtatious warmth of her voice as her great-
aunt had greeted Marcus chilled quite distinctly over her
own name, Lucy noticed cynically. Was there any woman
on the surface of the earth who was immune to Marcus's
personal brand of male charm?

'A truly delightful occasion, Alice. Thank you for inviting me.'

'My dear boy, how could I not? After all, your family have been taking care of our family's financial affairs since before the Peninsular War. Of course there should have been food, but I'm afraid Lucy rather let me down there.'

Lucy gasped in outrage.

'That— Ouch!' she protested as Marcus trod on her toes, then hustled her out into the street—just as though she were a prisoner under armed guard, Lucy decided indignantly.

'You do realise that you stood on my toes, don't you?' she objected, as she breathed in the familiar scent of the sun-warmed city.

'Better my foot on your toes than your foot in your own mouth, don't you think?' Marcus suggested.

It took Lucy several seconds to recognise what he was saying, but once she had she glowered indignantly and told him, 'It was Great-Aunt Alice herself who decided not to have any food. It was nothing to do with me.'

'You amaze me sometimes, you know, Lucy,' Marcus told her grimly. 'Has no one ever told you that a little tact goes a long way towards oiling the wheels of business and reputation?'

'You're a fine one to talk! You never bother using tact when you talk to me, do you?'

'Some situations call for stronger measures,' Marcus answered grimly.

'If you mean my marriage—' Lucy began hotly, and then stopped.

Her marriage was just not something she felt safe discussing with Marcus. The last thing she wanted was to have him probing into the whys and wherefores of her relationship with Nick. There was no point in allowing herself to be drawn into an argument she already knew she was not going to win.

'You can let go of me now, Marcus,' Lucy hissed valiantly several seconds later, when he was still holding on to her. But Marcus ignored her, keeping a firm grip on her arm as he flagged down a taxi and then opened the door for her, almost pushing her inside it. Lucy resentfully moved as far away from him as she could as he sat down beside her.

'Where to, guv?' the taxi driver demanded.

'Wendover Square. Number twenty-one.'

'Arncott Street.'

They had both spoken together.

'Make yer mind up,' the cabbie complained.

'Wendover Square,' Marcus repeated, before Lucy could speak, leaving her to glower angrily at him.

'It would have been easier if he'd dropped me off first, Marcus.'

'I want to talk to you,' Marcus told her coolly.

'So talk,' she said recklessly.

'In private,' Marcus informed her in a very gritty voice.

The taxi driver was turning into Wendover Square, its elegant Georgian houses overlooking one of London's most attractive private squares.

Marcus's house—the same house his grandfather and his great-grandfather had lived in, in fact all his ancestors right back to the Carring who had first begun the bank in the days of the Peninsular War—had just about the best position in the whole square. Four storeys high and double fronted, with a proper back garden, it was a true family house, and Lucy could see how impressed the cabbie was as he pulled up outside it and unlocked the door for them.

'I do hope that whatever you want to say to me isn't going to take too long, Marcus.' Lucy was trying to sound as businesslike as possible—a difficult task when suddenly, for no discernible reason, her tongue seemed to be slipping and sliding over her words, and the motion of the taxi had made her feel very dizzy indeed.

'No Mrs Crabtree?' she managed to articulate, when Marcus opened the door and there was no sign of his housekeeper. As Lucy knew, the woman treated her employer as though he were at the very most one step down from god status.

'She's gone to stay with her daughter, to help look after her new baby.'

'Oh!' Lucy gave an exclamation of surprise as she semi-stumbled in the hallway.

'I told you you'd had too much to drink,' Marcus said grimly. 'And you're certainly in no fit state to go anywhere on your own.'

His accusation stung—and all the more so because it was just not true. She didn't drink! But before she could say so, he was continuing curtly, 'You're out of touch, Lucy. The tipsy, thirty-something, Bridget Jones-type female is over. The in thing now is the committed working mother with two children and a husband—and if you don't believe me take a look at your own friends. Carly and Julia are both married now, and both mothers.'

As though she needed reminding of that! Lucy thought miserably.

'I am not thirty-anything,' she told him crossly instead. 'And, just in case you had forgotten, I've been married.'

'*Forgotten?* How the hell could anyone forget that?'

'And I have not had too much to drink,' Lucy added forcefully.

The look Marcus gave her made her whole body burn, never mind just her face.

'No? Well, all I can say is that if this is the state you were in when Nick Blayne picked you up, it's no wonder—'

'It's no wonder what?' Lucy stopped him. 'No wonder that I went to bed with him? Well, for your information, I went to bed with him because—'

'Spare me your reminiscences about how much you loved him, Lucy,' Marcus told her flatly. 'Blayne saw you coming and took advantage of you—financially, emotionally, and for all I know sexually as well. He used you, Lucy, and you let him. Couldn't you see what he was?' he demanded in exasperation. 'I should have thought even a sixteen-year-old virgin could have recognised that the man was a user.'

'Sixteen-year-old virgins probably have better eyesight than twenty-plus unmarrieds,' Lucy retaliated flippantly. How many times had she used flippancy as her defence against the powerful blasts of Marcus's irritated broadsides? Surely more than enough to know how much they increased his ire. But what else could she do? Without her protective shield of nonchalance she might just break down into a sobbing wreck of pleading female misery, and he would like that even less!

'I loved Nick,' she lied wildly.

'Did you? Or did you just want to go to bed with him?'

'A girl doesn't have to marry a man in order to have sex with him these days, Marcus. She doesn't even have to love him. All she needs to do is simply do it.'

She could see the contempt flashing through his eyes as he looked at her.

'Have you any idea just how provocative that statement is? Or how vulnerable you are?'

Lucy stared at him. 'What do you mean?'

'I mean that right now *any* man could get you into his bed.'

'That is so not true!'

'No? Want me to prove it to you?'

'You couldn't,' Lucy objected recklessly.

'No?'

He reached for her so suddenly that she didn't even have time to think about evading him, never mind actually do so. One minute she was standing in his hallway, the next she was in Marcus's arms, held securely against him. His mouth came down on her own, hard and sure, hot with male pride and anger, and he took her half-parted lips in a victor's kiss. And she didn't care, she didn't care one little bit. A feeling far more potent than the bubbles from a thousand bottles of champagne hit her emotions. He was kissing her. Marcus was kissing her.

Marcus was *kissing* her.

Marcus was kissing her!

CHAPTER THREE

'OH. MMM. Oh...' Greedily Lucy clung, both to the sensation and to the man delivering it, reaching up to wrap her arms tightly around Marcus's neck as she caved in to her own need. She had wanted him too much and for too long to resist this...this miracle of miracles, she decided headily, and she moved even closer to him, trying to ease the ache deep inside her body by arching into him and moving her body against his.

'Oh, Marcus...' she sighed ecstatically, as she felt the unmistakable surge of his erection pressing into her.

'Lucy...no!' He pushed her sharply away.

Bereft and stunned, she stared reproachfully at him.

'You see, this is exactly the kind of situation I've brought you here to avoid,' he told her brusquely. 'If I'd let you make your own way home—'

'But what if I don't want to avoid it?' Lucy demanded provocatively. 'What if I want...' What on earth was she saying? Another minute and she'd be telling Marcus that this was what she had been dreaming from the first time she had stood opposite him in his office. Dreaming of, lusting after, longing for...

'Never mind what you want,' Marcus told her acerbically. 'What you need right now is to sleep off that champagne.'

Reddening and humiliated, Lucy started to walk towards the door. 'Well, in that case I'd better go home, then, hadn't I?' she said petulantly. The truth was that, whilst she wasn't drunk, the glass and a half of champagne she'd

had was a whole glass more than she normally had to
drink—on an empty stomach, too. And there was no doubt
that the combined effect of Marcus's presence, the privacy
of his house, plus the intensity of her feelings for him were
all working together to make her want to put into practice
the feverish lust-filled desires she had kept hidden for so
very long. However, dizzy with lust and longing though
she was, she was still in control enough to recognise that
the best place for her right now was somewhere with a
comfortable bed and no Marcus.

'No way.' Marcus stopped her. 'You can sleep it off
here. Come on—this way.'

He had turned her round and was practically frog-
marching her up the stairs, Lucy recognised wrathfully.
She tried to pull away from him, and to her chagrin over-
balanced on her spindly heels.

'Right—that's it,' Marcus announced, swinging her up
into his arms before she could stop him as he climbed the
last couple of stairs.

With her face buried against his shoulder, and her hand
splayed out across his shirt, perfectly able to feel the crisp
male hair beneath it, Lucy felt as though she had suddenly
become a sort of sexual Lucy in Wonderland, fallen into
a magical fantasy world.

Still carrying her, Marcus strode down the landing and
in true Hollywood hero fashion pushed open a bedroom
floor with one highly polished shoe. How typical of
Marcus that he would wear such traditional-looking shoes,
Lucy acknowledged, whilst her stomach muscles cramped
in pleasure at the exciting discovery that said shoes looked
rather bigger than those worn by her unmourned ex-
husband. They must be at least a size eleven, maybe even
larger...

The room they were in was obviously a guest room,

pristinely neat and decorated in a rather old-fashioned and very unadventurous mix of traditional chintz and heavy inherited family furniture.

Not that Lucy had very much inclination to study the furniture—not when Marcus was sliding her down his body in such a delicious and delirium-inducing way. Sliding her down his body and trying to step back from her, she recognised. But she wasn't going to let him.

The shock of her own thoughts was a powerful adrenaline surge, filling her with a determination that was turning her into someone she hardly recognised. Someone who was demanding to know why she should not have what she wanted; why she should not do as others did and simply take what she wanted. Why she should not for once in her life simply put herself and her own needs first.

She had never experienced anything so alluringly tempting, so wonderfully empowering, so overwhelming irresistible. Why should she try to resist it? Why shouldn't she seize this opportunity? Why shouldn't she allow herself to seduce Marcus into taking her to bed? Why shouldn't she do what other women did all the time instead of denying herself what she so desperately wanted? Why should she always be the one to go without? Why shouldn't she allow herself this one night?

And tomorrow? When she had to face Marcus's anger and rejection?

But this wasn't tomorrow. It was today. It was here and now. She was already dealing with Marcus's rejection and had been for years. Why shouldn't she sweeten it with the kind of memories that would burn within the shrine of her most secret places for ever?

'Marcus... *Marcus*...' she whispered fiercely against his lips, and she lifted her mouth to his, wriggling as close to him as she could, oblivious to the fact that her movements had caused the press-studs fastening her fragile silk dress to pop open until she felt the unwanted presence of its small cap sleeves halfway down her arms.

The unwanted intrusion of her dress and its unfamiliarly draped sleeves was easily dealt with. She simply dropped her arms and let it slide down to the floor, to pool round her feet, then stepped out of it. Thus freed, she lifted her arms and wrapped them tightly round Marcus's neck, standing in only one shoe, a thin silk camisole and matching fluted-legged brief French knickers. Ridiculously, perhaps, one of the first things she had done after Nick's betrayal and their subsequent divorce was to go inside the Agent Provocateur shop she walked past most days on her way to her office and treat herself to the kind of underwear that every sensual woman had a right to enjoy—even if her husband had labelled her as sexless.

Marcus was trying to say something to her, she realised, as she rubbed her nose against the bare flesh of his throat with open sensual pleasure, breathing in the scent of him. And she could feel his fingers biting into the soft skin of her upper arms, too. But she was too lost in the sheer wonder of the moment, and what was happening, to pay any attention to what he might be trying to say. Why speak, after all, when they could be doing this? Lucy decided giddily in adrenaline- and love-fuelled need, as she created around herself the familiar fantasy that had comforted her Marcus-deprived body for so long. The fantasy in which Marcus just could not resist her and didn't even want to. Poor Marcus. He was probably dreadfully uncomfortable in all those clothes—that tie, that buttoned-up shirt—surely it behoved her to aid him with their removal?

She tried for the tie first, her tongue-tip pressed firmly against her teeth as she worked at the knot with eager fingers.

'Lucy!'

'Mmm?' She had worn a tie at school, as part of her uniform, so surely unknotting this one...?

'Lucy...' Marcus's hands covered her own. Lucy looked up at him and gave him an approving smile. Obviously he shared her own eagerness for him to be rid of his clothes and wanted to help her. She intended to say as much to him, but suddenly she became distracted as she looked at his mouth, and then she couldn't look away again.

'Marcus.' She whispered his name in dizzy delight as she looked at it and longed for it, touching her own tongue to her lips as her eyes darkened with the heat of her own hunger for him.

Reaching up, she pressed her mouth tenderly against his. His lips felt firm and strong, his flesh sensuously distracting and hunger-inducing as she breathed tiny kisses against it, little nibbles that grew bolder as each taste fuelled her need for more. Marcus's hands left her arms and gripped her waist.

It was nice to be held so tightly, she acknowledged, but it would be even nicer if he were to touch her breast. So much easier, surely, for her to simply take his hand and place it against the warm swell of her own flesh beneath the thin silk of her cami and hold it there whilst her tongue darted excitedly against the closed line of his mouth, begging for entrance to the pleasures that lay beyond them...

'Lucy!'

What was Marcus doing? He couldn't be pushing her away. Frantically she reached out to him, then lost her balance and started to fall backwards onto the bed behind her.

Immediately Marcus made a grab for her, but it was too late, and somehow or other she was lying on the bed, with Marcus on top of her. The full weight of his body was pressing her down into the mattress and it felt so good. In fact it felt, *he* felt like heaven...like everything good she had ever experienced in the whole of her life, only ten times more than that. She exhaled in delighted bliss and wrapped her arms tightly round his neck, pressing her mouth against his, her lips parted invitingly.

She heard Marcus make a thick muffled sound. Surely not a groan? And then his hands were in her hair, his fingers hard and warm against her scalp as he held her head in sensual imprisonment and his mouth moved on hers.

Had she imagined she knew what a kiss was? She had known nothing—less than nothing, Lucy admitted, as the emotional champagne bubbles of delight and disbelief exploded inside her and raced along her veins into every part of her body. Most especially to those bits of her body that were particularly receptive to the kind of pleasure Marcus was giving her. Even her toes were curling, in a silent exclamation of thrilled awe.

So this was what it felt like to be truly aroused by and responsive to a man. No wonder in times gone by mothers of impressionable daughters had guarded them so ferociously. Already she was hooked on what Marcus was giving her; already she wanted and needed more. His tongue-tip teased the sensitivity of her lips with small, almost whip-like tormenting caresses before suddenly hardening and thrusting deep into her mouth, not just once but repeatedly, until her whole body was shuddering in rhythmic response to those thrusts.

Dizzily Lucy reflected that she'd asked for one miracle but had actually got two! Was that how it worked with this miracle thing? Once you had tuned in to miracles, so to speak, did they just keep on coming? Little miracles popping up here, there and everywhere?

'Oh, I do so hope there will be more,' she whispered ecstatically as Marcus released her mouth.

'What?' he demanded, looking down at her, all blazing impatience and irritation and lethal male desire.

'More,' she repeated sweetly, giving him a beatific smile. 'I would like more, Marcus. Much more,' she emphasised.

'You want more?' he repeated.

Why was he looking at her like that? As though he couldn't believe what he was hearing? As though the hard pulse of his erection didn't exist?

Lucy wasn't going to let herself be dragged out of her fantasy.

'Oh, yes,' she agreed. Now that he had kissed her, and she had tasted him, her body was so fixated on him that it would probably mount an all-out rebellion if it was denied him now. She wanted him and she was going to have him, she decided firmly. She deserved to have him.

'It's been such a long time, you see,' she told him. And it had. Such a very, very long time since she had first looked at him and wanted him. And now here was her very own personal miracle, making it possible for her to have him. So of *course* she wanted more of them—and of him, too. But right now she didn't have time to explain all of that to him because right now...right now she had far more important and exciting things she wanted to do.

She looked up into his eyes and then gave in to the temptation to stroke her tongue-tip along the line of his throat. She heard him groan, felt him shudder, and then his hands were on her body, as she had so much longed for them to be, cupping her breasts whilst she tugged off his tie and her fingers worked busily to unfasten the buttons of his shirt. The pads of his thumbs were stroking her erect nipples, working the silk of her camisole against them until she moaned in helpless delight at the effect his deliberate stroking of the fine silk against her sensitive flesh was having on her.

But she got her own back. She had unfastened his shirt and was free to slide her hands inside it, palms flat against the hard muscle of his chest. She lifted her head and kissed his collarbone, stringing tiny kisses together in mute arousal. His fingers plucked erotically at one nipple whilst her own urgent movements brought the other free of her cami. She flicked her tongue-tip urgently against the small stone hardness of Marcus's flat male nipples, tasting first one and then the other, tormenting herself with the knowledge of the pleasure that lay ahead of her when she allowed her hands and her mouth to move down over his body.

Marcus bent his head and kissed her throat. His fingertip traced the shape of her ear whilst his teeth nibbled gently on her lobe, and then his mouth caressed the flesh just behind it. A spasm of intense pleasure and longing shot through her, and she arched her back to bring her breast fully into his hand, a small, keening moan bubbling in her throat. Her toes curled, and automatically she opened her legs in eager supplication.

Against her body she could feel the erect heat and hardness of Marcus's own arousal, whilst what he was doing to that tiny spot of flesh was practically bringing her to the point of orgasm all by itself.

His hand stroked her hip and then slid lower, finding the soft curve of her bottom beneath the wide silky leg of her fluted French knickers. Some women thought thongs were sexy, but right now Lucy felt that what she was wearing and the access to all areas they gave Marcus was far more alluring. Without any need to remove them, his hand had already moved from her bottom to the soft silky curls of hair between her legs, and his thumb was massaging slow circles against her mound before his fingers started to tease her open.

Lucy moaned and writhed and lifted her body up to his hands, then gasped as he stroked deftly into her wetness in the very same heartbeat as his lips started to caress her tight nipple.

She felt as though a magical cord was somehow stretched from her breast to her belly, and that what Marcus was doing to her was tightening it to the point where she wanted to scream with urgent longing for him to do more, to take her further, deeper.

'Marcus, I'm going to come,' she protested thickly. But instead of heeding her warning and removing his clothes, so that he could slide into her, he lifted his head and looked steadily at her whilst his fingers moved more purposefully over her. Over her and into her. Stroking her, teasing her, until she was so hot, and so wet, and so wanting...

'I'm not coming until you're inside me,' she told him, panting out the words as she struggled to hold back her orgasm, her fingers closing over him through the fabric of his clothes and her body shuddering violently in excitement as she realised how thick and strong he actually was.

He undressed with speedy efficiency, scarcely giving her time to enjoy the pleasure of looking at his naked body. Then he undressed her as well, and then positioned himself between her welcoming, eager thighs.

'Missionary position?' she huffed, pulling a small face.

'It's all we've got time for if you want me inside you when we come,' Marcus told her rawly, before bending his head to kiss her naked breasts in turn whilst he rubbed the hard hot head of his erection against her clitoris until she called out frantically to him, begging him to satisfy her.

Lucy felt her orgasm seize her in its seismic grip with his third thrust, her muscles fastening round him to hold and caress him, to draw from him the sharp, sweet juice of life itself.

She knew the moment she opened he eyes that she wasn't in her own bed. But it was several seconds before she realised just whose bed she was in—or rather whose bedroom, since the room she was in was obviously a guest room. Marcus's guest room. In Marcus's Wendover Square house.

She gave a small despairing groan as the events of the previous afternoon and evening formed images inside her head—images she was forced to view without the protection of her earlier adrenaline-induced armour.

What on earth had possessed her to behave like that? Granted, she loved Marcus, and always would love him, but last night she had... She swallowed uncomfortably whilst her whole body burned in the flames of her own shocking memories.

She looked at her watch. Ten a.m.

She shot upright in the bed. It couldn't possibly be! She'd always woken up at seven at the very latest—always. Even on her honeymoon.

But last night with Marcus she'd had the kind of sex, the quality of sex that she most definitely had not had with Nick—either on her honeymoon or at any other time.

Marcus? Where was he? She hauled up the duvet, holding it to cover her naked breasts, even though some sixth sense told her that the house was a Marcus-free zone. Her clothes, which she could blush-makingly remember abandoning all over the place, had been thoughtfully retrieved and neatly folded—although she couldn't see her knickers—and there was an envelope propped up on the tallboy with her name written across it in Marcus's imperious hand. Keeping the duvet wrapped around herself, she got out of bed and padded over to the tallboy. Inside the envelope was a piece of paper on which Marcus had written economically.

Your underwear is in the dryer. Don't leave without having some breakfast—coffee, fruit, cereal, etc, in cupboards and fridge. Will be in touch this p.m. re visit to Beatrice.

Her knickers were in the dryer! How domestic, how authoritarian—how Marcus.

And how lovely to know they would be clean. If she had one tiny little hang-up, it was that she was almost too neat and tidy—and everything that went with that, Lucy admitted as she hurried into the bathroom. But then boarding school did that to a person, she reflected, as she stood beneath the refreshing sting of the shower, lathering her skin and her hair.

The décor in Marcus's house might be slightly old-fashioned, but the guest bathroom was well stocked with everything that an overnight visitor minus her sponge bag might need. Lucy smiled approvingly when she found a new toothbrush as well as toothpaste in the basket beside the basin, along with a new comb, a small unopened jar of face cream and even deodorant.

Fortunately her hair was naturally straight, so she had no need to do anything other than wash and comb it, knowing that by the time she reached her office it would have dried. And even more fortunately, given the time and the fact that she had a considerable amount of paperwork to attend to, she could go straight there and change into a pair of jeans once she got there. She always kept several changes of clothes there, just in case.

Her head had begun to ache unpleasantly—a combination of anxiety about what Marcus might be likely to say to her about last night and lack of caffeine, Lucy decided as she made her way downstairs in her silk dress but minus her stiletto shoes.

Marcus's kitchen was, of course, immaculate. Having retrieved her underwear from the laundry room and quickly put it on—no matter how saucy it might be, she simply was not a 'no knickers' girl, Lucy decided firmly— she hurried into the kitchen, desperately in need of a very strong cup of coffee.

Ten minutes later, after going through every cupboard and finding only decaf, she was forced to admit that there was an unbridgeable gap between her idea of what constituted a proper breakfast drink and Marcus's.

Decaf. She screwed up her nose in distaste as she made herself a cup and munched half-heartedly on a banana.

Those butterflies in her stomach weren't there just because she needed her caffeine fix. They were there because last night she had seduced Marcus. Because she had thrown herself at him—and onto him. Her face started to burn, and not just with the guilty embarrassment she ought to be feeling. Her mental self might feel guilt and shame and be dreading having to face Marcus, but her physical self was positively crowing with delight, reliving with relish every single intimate caress and kiss. It certainly had no intention of feeling any kind of shame whatsoever.

But what about her emotional self? Lucy wondered sadly as she let herself out of the house, carefully checking that the door had locked behind her before setting off to walk the short distance to her Sloane Street office. Her emotional self was caught between the two opposing forces of her mind and her body. Her emotional self loved Marcus and yearned for him to love her back. Her mental self said that it was simply not possible, and warned her of the pain and humiliation she was courting. Her physical self, on the other hand, was still wallowing in the triumphant afterglow of sex with a lover who had elevated the experience to a plane hitherto unknown to her other than via fevered fantasies and lustful daydreams.

Add to all of that the fact that the thought of seeing Marcus again was making her feel physically sick with apprehension, and it was no wonder her head was pounding, Lucy decided as she hurried into the coffee shop she regularly used to obtain her daytime caffeine fix. To her relief she was the only customer.

'Your usual?' the girl behind the counter asked cheerfully.

'Please, Sarah—no, make that two,' Lucy told her. 'And a couple of chocolate brownies as well.'

Sarah gave her a wicked grin.

'Caffeine and carbs? It must have been a good night last night.'

'The best—at least what I can remember of it,' Lucy agreed, rolling her eyes and grinning back. But the truth was that the first bit of her light-hearted response to Sarah's teasing was exactly that—the truth. It had been the best—and was likely to remain so, she reminded herself grimly as she gathered up her double espressos and her brownies and stepped back into the late-morning sunshine.

Marcus would certainly not want a rerun, and now that she had had her fantasies come to life—now that she knew just how far short they had fallen of the reality of the heaven of Marcus's arms around her, Marcus's mouth on hers, Marcus's lovemaking—she was going to have to spend the rest of her life not just knowing she could never love anyone else but also knowing that she was never going to want to have sex with anyone else.

It was a miserable thing to have to admit to herself as she hurried into the building that housed Prêt a Party's offices, pausing to exchange smiles with Harry the doorman as she did so.

Once, Prêt a Party's offices had been filled with the busy hum of telephones ringing, clients calling, the laughter of her two best friends and partners. But now they were empty and silent. Kicking the door closed as she balanced her coffee, Lucy fought the temptation not to think about how Marcus had kicked the bedroom door open last night—and what had happened after he had.

Five minutes later, her dress exchanged for a tee shirt and a pair of jeans, and her French knickers carefully parcelled up to be rewashed and kept as a very personal souvenir, Lucy savoured the last delicious gulp of coffee whilst she scrolled down her e-mails.

No new requests for Prêt a Party's services, she saw gloomily. The only commission she had pending was the sportswear manufacturer's launch of a new football boot, which was to be held at a very trendy nightclub of the type favoured by TV celebs, models, premier league footballers and the like.

Everything was already in place for the launch, but while she drank her second coffee Lucy brought up the worksheets for it to check them over.

She had based the whole event on the manufacturer's logo and colours, playing on a 'team event' theme, since they were launching a football boot. Cheerleaders dressed in a highly-sexed version of a football strip would provide the main entertainment by chanting the client's name, a new cocktail was going to be served, and Lucy had decided that the food was going to be miniature portions of that favourite laddish treat—curry and chips in a plastic carton.

When her telephone suddenly rang she stared at it apprehensively. Marcus. It had to be! She picked up the receiver and flicked her tongue nervously over her dry lips.

'May I speak to the Honourable Lucy Blayne, please?'

How was it possible for her heart to sink with relief? Lucy wondered, as she corrected her caller discreetly by responding, 'Lucy Cardrew speaking.'

'Oh, hi. It's Andrew Walker here—your cousin Johnny...'

Andrew Walker. The miracle who might be going to save Prêt a Party and what was left of her trust fund.

'Oh, yes—of course!'

'Look, I know it's short notice, but I'm going to be out of the country from tomorrow, so I wondered if there was any chance that you might be free for lunch today so that we could talk things over and set the ball rolling, so to speak.'

Lucy looked at her watch. It was gone twelve now.

'I could make a late lunch at half one?' she suggested.

'Great. Is the Brasserie in Pont Street okay for you?'

'Perfect,' Lucy confirmed. Pont Street was virtually round the corner from her office, and the Brasserie was one of her favourite eateries.

'Excellent. I'll see you there at one-thirty, then.'

Replacing the receiver, Lucy looked down at her jeans. She would have to change them for something more suitable for a business lunch. The Armani suit, probably—referred to by her friends as 'the armour', because Lucy invariably wore it whenever she had a business meeting to attend. And always when she went to see Marcus to ask him to release more money from her trust fund.

CHAPTER FOUR

AT DEAD on one-thirty, fortified by two more cups of espresso and armoured with the Armani, Lucy fought her way past the untidy jumble of camera-toting, motorbike-riding paparazzi clustered boldly outside the Brasserie, waiting for its celeb diners to arrive and leave, and pushed open the door. She was immediately greeted with a welcoming smile from the receptionist, who recognised her.

'I'm having lunch with a Mr Walker—Andrew Walker?'

'Mr Walker is already here and waiting at the table,' the *maître d'* informed her.

'Oh, Angelo, you're back! How lovely. Did you have a wonderful time in Sydney with your son and grandchildren?' Lucy asked warmly.

'That boy—he is doing so well. He has his own restaurant now,' Angelo informed her proudly as he escorted her past the other tables to one set discreetly out of earshot of the others.

The man seated there stood up as she approached, extending his hand. 'Andrew Walker,' he introduced himself, and Lucy shook it and sat down.

'Hello Andrew—Lucy Cardrew.'

He was a middle-aged man of middle height with an unremarkable face. He was smartly if somewhat formally dressed, in a suit that—like those Marcus wore—had obviously come from a bespoke tailor. The shirt had all the hallmarks of its Jermyn Street origins, and his shoes were handmade too, but whereas Marcus always looked completely at home and at ease in the formality of his dark business suits and handmade shirts, Andrew Walker looked rather uncomfortable in his clothes, and they in turn looked new and somewhat alien to him.

As he signalled to the waiter he told Lucy, 'Your cousin will have already mentioned to you that I may be interested in investing in your business?'

'Yes,' Lucy acknowledged, thanking the waiter for the menu he was handing her and shaking her head when Andrew asked her what wine she would like.

'Just water for me,' she told the waiter firmly.

Andrew didn't resume talking about his plans until after they had been served with their food, and even then he kept his voice low and conspiratorial as he leaned across the table to tell her firmly, 'I must stress that at this stage it is imperative that you don't discuss my approach to you with anyone else.'

'But my solicitor will have to know, surely?' Lucy protested.

'Ultimately, perhaps. Although I would prefer it if my own solicitor drew up all the necessary agreements first.' He gave a small shrug. 'I have discovered that the success of my existing business has resulted in other people becoming very keen to find out what my future financial moves will be. Any market can only sustain a certain amount of business. How much business do you have in hand at the moment?'

'Very little,' Lucy told him honestly. 'I expect you know about the financial problems the business has had to face following my divorce?'

'Of course.'

'I've got a big event coming up next month—the launch of a new football boot—'

'And that kind of business is profitable?'

'Corporate business is hugely profitable compared with

private business,' Lucy explained. 'When I'm asked to organise an event where the client wants access to my address book, in order to ensure that they have enough
A-list celebs at the event to assure them of maximum press
coverage, I can charge more than when I am organising a
private event, where the guest list is supplied by the person
giving the event. Obviously any kind of launch is an event
when the attendance of the right kind of high-profile celebrities is a must. For this event, for instance, the client
is guaranteeing the attendance of the premier league football star who is the face of their brand, and I have sent
invitations to everyone in my address book who is guaranteed to bring the press to the event.'

'"Everyone" being...?'

Lucy gave a small shrug. 'Certain top-rank models and
soap stars—the top names, not the B-and C-list—a smat-
tering of It Girl-types and rock star offspring, plus some
of the more sociable dot-com millionaires. People who are
glamorous and newsworthy, and who will add lustre to the
event.'

'I see... So I take it that much of Prêt a Party's market
value lies in its address book?'

'In some ways,' Lucy agreed.

'When it comes to organising food and drink, venues,
flowers, that kind of thing, who is responsible for choosing
who will supply those?'

'Prêt a Party,' Lucy told him promptly. 'I'm very strict
about who I do and don't use. Prêt a Party's reputation has
been built on the quality of everything we provide—and
that includes the ancillary services we use, whether they
are marquees or food.'

'Mmm. Have you ever thought about selling the Prêt a
Party concept as a franchise?'

'No.'

'Well, that is one of the areas I am very interested in us looking into as business partners. It will be expensive to start with, of course, until the franchisee revenue starts to come in. But what I have in mind is to use the contacts I have already made via my turnkey business to build up our own ancillary service agencies—so that we can supply our franchisees with everything they need and the Prêt a Party guarantee of quality. We buy our own marquees and we provide the men to erect them. We supply the waiters, the glasses and the drinks. We provide the florists and the musicians and the cleaning staff—in fact, we supply everything and anything else our franchisees and their clients may need.'

Lucy stared at him, her food forgotten. 'That's *brilliant*,' she told him, her eyes shining. 'But it will cost a fortune...'

'Indeed it will. But I think the eventual return will make it a worthwhile investment.'

Lucy didn't know what to say. The most she had been hoping for had been an injection of capital to refloat the business so that she could build it up again, but what Andrew Walker was talking about so matter-of-factly was the creation of a whole business empire.

'As I've already said, I would like your assurance that what we are discussing is kept strictly between the two of us at this stage.'

Lucy nodded her head.

'I'd like to get things moving as quickly as possible, but obviously you're going to need time to think over my proposal. How would you feel about us meeting up again when I get back from this trip?'

'That...That sounds fine,' Lucy managed to tell him, as she fought to sound businesslike and professional rather than giddy with the delight and relief she was actually feeling.

'Here's my card,' Andrew Walker told her. 'I have just bought a new property in Holland Park. It's in the course of being renovated at the moment, but once the renovations are finished I intend to throw a large party there for my friends and my business contacts. If all goes as I hope it will, that event will be organised by Prêt a Party, and will be a means of introducing our new joint venture to everyone.'

'*Brilliant,*' Lucy repeated, and meant it.

It was three o'clock before Lucy got back to her office, her head buzzing with excited thoughts and plans. She could scarcely believe her good luck, and all because Andrew had happened to see that spread about Prêt a Party in *A-List Life*.

The only down side to this wonderful piece of good luck was that she wasn't going to be able to say anything about it to Marcus. Or at least not just yet. It would be such a relief to know that she didn't have to plead with him to change his mind and allow her to use what was left of her trust fund to clear Prêt a Party's overdraft and give her some much-needed working capital. She looked at the telephone. There was no message from Marcus, despite the fact that he had said he would be in touch with her. Had he changed his mind? Had he been thinking about last night and decided that he simply never wanted to see her again, just in case she tried to repeat her behaviour?

And if he did ring what was he likely to say?

She needed an espresso, Lucy decided.

Marcus frowned as he studied the view from his office window. His father, grandfather, great-grandfather and all those who had gone before them had occupied this office in their turn, and Marcus had known from the moment he had been old enough to know such things that one day he would have to take over responsibility for the bank and its clients. His father's death when Marcus had been only six years old had meant that Marcus had been brought up by his mother and grandfather, who'd made sure that Marcus was aware of how important the bank was, and the fact that he was expected to dedicate his life to it. At twenty-one, fresh from university, Marcus had resented that responsibility, and the way that life had forced it on him, even while he had felt honour-bound to accept it. His grandfather at nearly eighty had needed to be allowed to retire, and he had a duty to take over from him.

And so he had put aside his dreams of travelling the world and focused instead on doing what he had to do.

He was nearly six years older than Lucy, and the first time she had walked into his office his feelings towards her had been a mixture of irritation and impatience. Irritation because he'd had enough on his plate without having to act as her trustee, and impatience because he had seen in her eyes the dazed look of a young woman about to develop a huge and unwanted crush on him.

Marcus did not consider himself to be vain. But he had had enough relationships to know what the look Lucy had given him meant. He might have had no choice other than to do what was expected of him and take over the bank, but he had grimly and determinedly held on to what independence he did have. Marriage, so far as he was concerned, was a necessary evil he wanted to put off for as long as he could. One day, yes, he would marry, and provide the bank with its future administrator, but not yet. And he certainly had no intention of ever allowing himself to fall in love.

His mouth hardened. Marcus had seen at first hand the destruction 'falling in love' could cause. His own father had fallen in love when Marcus was six, and he had left his wife—Marcus's mother—abandoning her and his two children because of that 'love'. He had destroyed their family and left Marcus feeling betrayed and bereft. And, since he had not been able to hate the father he had loved so much, his six-year-old mind had turned its hatred on the emotion that had caused him to leave instead.

Three weeks after he had left them Marcus's father had been killed in an accident—along with his lover. Marcus had mourned him and promised himself that he would never make the same mistake as his father. He would never, ever allow himself to fall in love. Because of that he had made sure that the women he dated, the women he slept with, were sophisticated, slightly older than he was himself, often post-divorce and pre-second marriage. Women who enjoyed sex and were socially aware, women who understood the rules of the game as he chose to play it—women, in short, who were the complete opposite of Lucy.

Over the years the initial irritation and impatience he had felt towards Lucy had fused together to become a gut reaction which was activated every time he saw her, and it had been intensified to the point where it had been laced with incredulous disbelief and anger when she had married Nick Blayne.

She was supposed to be an intelligent young woman. She must have been able to see what Nick Blayne was. But she had obviously been too blinded by 'love' to care. Love and lust, if the newspaper photographs he had seen of her cavorting half naked with Blayne on the Caribbean island where she had first met him were anything to go by.

Irritation, impatience, anger—and, if he was honest with himself, perhaps a touch of guilt?

Guilt? What the hell did he have to feel guilty about? He hadn't been responsible for her marrying Blayne, or the catastrophic events that had followed. He had done everything within his power to stop Lucy destroying her own financial security and allowing her now ex-husband to plunder the trust fund, but she had refused to listen to him.

But, ridiculously, he did feel guilty. And for some reason that made him feel even more intensely irritated and angry with Lucy.

He was, he reminded himself grimly, her trustee, and he was now ruthlessly determined to protect what was left of her inheritance—from Lucy herself, if that should prove necessary.

He was well aware that her original blushing, bashful self-consciousness and virginal sexual curiosity about him had turned to resentment edged with apprehension. He had made it clear to her that he was not going to be persuaded into allowing her to remove what was left of her trust fund to put into her ailing business, no matter how much pressure she put on him to do so.

Prêt a Party was suffering the natural death throes of a business ruined by greed and mismanagement. The only thing that could save it now was a massive injection of capital and a very firm hand grasping its control. That had translated in Marcus's mind into *his* massive capital injection and *his* firm hand, but whilst he could quite easily spare the money, he could not spare the time to salvage the wreckage of Lucy's once profitable business.

He had stood by and watched—first assessingly, then reluctantly and then grudgingly admiringly—as she built up Prêt a Party into a very nice little business, even if she had continued to irritate him with her almost aggressive post-crush antagonism towards him and her refusal to listen to his advice.

But all that had been before last night! Taking Lucy to bed had been the last thing on his mind when he had removed her from the party.

But he had done so. And now...

Marcus frowned heavily. He was almost thirty-five years old—an age by which all his male ancestors had already been married and had fathered the male heir who would ultimately take over the family bank. Since he had never been in love, it was hard for Marcus to envisage what being 'in love' might feel like. His observations of love in others inclined him to the view that he was better off not knowing. He had deliberately chosen relationships which allowed him to avoid marriage, but at the same time he had known that ultimately he must marry. And over this last year he had become increasingly aware of his duty to the bank and to the past. He needed a wife and he needed an heir.

Finding a wife would not be a problem, but finding the right kind of wife—who would adapt to his way of life and understand the duties and responsibilities it carried—could be one. Especially when the kind of marriage he wanted was one based on practicality rather than emotion. Especially when one considered his wish to father an heir.

It was time for him to find himself a woman. A woman with whom he was both socially and sexually compatible. A woman, perhaps, like Lucy.

Lucy? Had he gone mad? She exasperated him as no other woman could, and her marriage to Nick Blayne had only increased his impatient anger towards her.

But last night she had enticed and aroused him as no other woman had.

The truth was that Lucy needed protecting from herself.

He would certainly be a far safer and more suitable husband for her than another Nick Blayne. A marriage between them would benefit them both. He needed a wife, and Lucy certainly needed a husband—if only to prevent her from repeating the mistake she had made in marrying Blayne.

And Lucy loved children.

Actually, for them to marry one another was in many ways entirely logical. She understood the world he lived in because it was also her world. They both wanted children, and sexually he had sown all the wild oats he wanted to sow—even if a part of him still mourned the loss of his youthful dreams of travel and adventure.

His mind was made up, Marcus decided abruptly. He intended to marry Lucy. And the sooner the better.

All he had to do now was find a way to convince her that she needed to marry him. And Marcus though he knew exactly how to do that.

The sensuality Lucy had displayed last night had surprised him, as had the pleasurable intensity of her sexual response to him. Lucy was a woman with a warm sex drive, a woman currently without a sexual partner in her life and quite clearly a woman who wanted one.

All he had to do was make her need work in his favour, Marcus decided coolly. He walked over to his desk and picked up the telephone receiver.

The message light was flashing on her telephone when Lucy walked back into the office. She had been longer at the coffee shop than she had expected. Her heart slalomed the length of her chest cavity before skidding dangerously to a halt as she played the message and heard Marcus's voice, telling her that he had arranged for them to visit his sister and that he would pick her up from her office at four o'clock.

Four o'clock? It was ten to now, Lucy saw, panic-stricken.

Thirteen and a half minutes later she was on her way downstairs, her hair combed, her lips glossed, and her heart thudding like a drum beat.

'There you are—come on. There's a traffic warden on the prowl and I don't want to get a ticket.'

There was no time to object as Marcus took hold of her arm and hurried over to the Bentley parked illegally out-side the office block, opening the passenger door for her so that she could scramble in whilst he strode round to the driver's door.

The interior of the car smelled of leather and Marcus, and Lucy leaned back in her seat and closed her eyes, breathing as slowly and carefully as she could.

'Our flight leaves at six—which means you've just about got time to pack if I drive you back to your flat now.'

'What? What flight? Where are we going?' Her eyes snapped open and she lurched forward in her seat.

'To see Beatrice, of course,' Marcus told her patiently. 'Remember? You're going to advise her about organising a party for George's fiftieth.'

'Your sister lives in Chelsea!' Lucy protested dizzily.

'Most of the time, yes. But she and George also have a villa in Majorca, and that's where she is right now. She thought it would be a good idea if you flew out to see her while she's there, so that she can discuss George's party with you while he isn't around. She doesn't want him to guess what's going on.'

Silently Lucy digested what he was saying to her. It was not particularly unusual for clients to fly her out to all manner of places, in order to consult her or to get her opinion of their chosen venue for their event, but Marcus had said very clearly '*our* flight', which meant...

'You're going to Majorca as well?' she demanded.

'I have some family business I need to discuss with Beatrice, so she suggested we might as well travel out together,' Marcus told her calmly. 'We'll be staying for a couple of days, so you'll need to pack a few things.'

'And I'll have to get changed. I can't travel to Palma wearing armour,' Lucy protested.

'Armour?'

Lucy could feel herself going red at she recognised her slip-up.

'It's what I call my business suit,' she mumbled.

She could feel Marcus looking at her, but his only comment was a very dry, 'Mmm.'

Marcus turned into Sloane Square and then cut through a couple of narrow back streets before finally bringing the Bentley to a halt in a conveniently empty parking space right outside the block of flats where she lived.

'I'll come up with you.'

It was a statement, not a question or an offer.

Wasn't Marcus going to say *anything* about last night? She had been dreading seeing him all day, worrying about what he would say and how she could respond.

She had told herself that the worst-case scenario would be if he had simply guessed the truth and challenged her with it. She had even rehearsed the scene mentally inside her head to prepare herself.

Marcus would say: You're in love with me, aren't you?
Lucy: What? Certainly not. What on earth makes you think that I could be?

Marcus—in that horrid dry voice he could use to such dramatic effect: Last night?

Lucy—breezily, looking amused and nonchalant: Oh, that! Good heavens, no. I just fancied a shag, that's all.

But evidently that wasn't going to be how it happened.

Leaving Marcus to follow her, Lucy hurried past the concierge with a quick 'hello' and then up the stairs. Her flat was on the first floor, and tiny, but at least she owned it outright and it wasn't a drain on her finances—unlike the much grander flat Nick had insisted on them renting during their marriage.

She unlocked the door and walked into the small hall-way. The enclosed and windowless space had been made larger and brighter by the addition of two non-matching mirrors she had 'borrowed' from the attics at home. A small table, also rescued from attic oblivion, which she had painted cream just like the walls, stood under one of the mirrors. On it Lucy had arranged not flowers, since she believed that every living thing needed natural light and proper fresh air, but instead her precious Jo Malone scented candles and a collection of glass candlesticks. Would Marcus notice the tasteful effect of the arrangement as he followed her into the hallway?

Beyond the hallway lay a tiny sitting room, furnished and decorated in various shades of cream, and pin-neat.

'Before I do anything else I'm going to make myself a cup of coffee,' Lucy told Marcus. 'Would you like a cup?'

'No, thanks. We don't have very much time, you know,' he reminded her.

'You're the one who's organised this, not me, and I'm not going anywhere until I've had my caffeine fix,' Lucy informed him stubbornly, heading for the kitchen.

'Fine! Where do you keep your passport, Lucy?'

'In the bureau behind the sofa,' Lucy told him from the kitchen.

Marcus opened the bureau and saw passports immediately. Two of them were bundled together inside a rubber band. He snapped off the band and opened the top one, and then wished that he hadn't. It was the passport Lucy had had when she had been married, and the photograph inside it showed a bright-eyed, happy-looking young woman. Her current passport, though—the one she had obtained after her divorce, when she had reverted to her maiden name—showed a thinner-faced young woman whose eyes held stark pain and despair. What on earth had she seen in Nick Blayne? How could she have loved him? Was it really *'loved'*?

'Did you find the passport?' Lucy asked as she walked past him with her coffee and pushed open her bedroom door. Lifting a small case from beneath the bed onto it, she began methodically opening drawers and placing what she thought she would need on her bed.

'Look—while you're doing that, why don't I pack your toiletries for you?'

Having Marcus safely out of the way and out of her line of vision, instead of standing there watching her and making her think about last night, was a very good idea, Lucy acknowledged. So she nodded her head and handed him the bag she used for such necessities, exhaling slowly when he had disappeared into her small bathroom.

Determinedly Lucy started to fold the things she had put on the bed, and place them into the flat packs she always used for travelling.

'Lucy, what about your pills?' Marcus called out from the bathroom.

Her pills! Thank heavens he had reminded her. She had learned the hard way never to go anywhere without her sun allergy pills.

'In the cabinet,' she called back. 'Second shelf down, right-hand side.'

She heard him opening the cabinet door as she placed the flat packs in her case, and then he called out again, 'I can't find them.'

Putting down the pack she was holding, Lucy walked into the bathroom, holding her breath when she was forced to squeeze past him to reach the cabinet.

'They're right here,' she told him, taking the allergy tablets from the shelf.

'Those aren't contraceptive pills,' Marcus objected.

Contraceptive pills?

'No. I don't take contraceptive pills. I don't need to. I've never needed to. Nick always used a condom. It was something he was obsessive about. He told me that he never had and never would have sex without wearing one.'

This wasn't a subject she wanted to discuss with Marcus in any way, shape or form, Lucy recognised. But she couldn't help wondering if the fact that Marcus had felt so good inside her last night had been because he had been inside her skin to skin, and she had loved the intimacy of knowing that.

As Lucy hurried back into the bedroom Marcus frowned. Last night, with unprecedented recklessness, the last thing on his mind had been the need for any kind of contraceptive or health precaution. He had to admit that hearing Lucy's ex-husband had insisted on wearing a condom was very good news.

He watched her whilst she finished her packing. He could feel his body tightening, and a very specific ache gripping it. He wanted her.

He was supposed to be focusing on getting her to want him, not allowing himself to want her.

'Ready?' he demanded tersely.

Lucy gave an unsmiling nod of assent.

CHAPTER FIVE

PALMA airport was always busy, and today was no exception. Lucy struggled to dodge the mounds of luggage and keep up with Marcus who, despite having their luggage to deal with, still somehow or other managed to have a positively 'parting of the Red Sea' effect on the crowds. They opened to allow him through, and then closed again, forcing her to fight her way through.

Marcus had now reached the exit, where he was being approached by two pretty girls wearing the uniforms of a certain car rental firm. Was it a car they were hoping to persuade him to hire, or a date they were hoping to be offered? Lucy wondered jealously as she finally caught up with him.

'I was just explaining to these ladies that the hotel will have sent a car to collect us,' he told Lucy.

'The hotel? What hotel?' Lucy demanded as he started to walk towards the waiting chauffeurs with their boards displaying clients' names. 'I thought we were staying with Beatrice.'

'Did you? The villa's quite small and remote, and since Beatrice is there to oversee some remedial work on the bathrooms I didn't think it was a good idea for us to expect her to put us up. I've booked us into a hotel instead. It's in Deia, very close to the Residencia, and supposed to be even better. And don't worry about the bill. I shall be paying it. Ah, there's our driver.'

If she stood on her tiptoes, she could just about see the

smartly uniformed chauffeur holding up a placard that read 'Hotel Boutique, Deia'.

Lucy knew Majorca quite well, since it had recently become very much one of the 'in' places to stay, following on from various celebs buying property in an exclusive enclave of villas and boutique hotels that had sprung up on a previously undeveloped part of the island's coastline. The Residencia had been *the* place to stay in this upmarket resort, and from what she had heard the new Hotel Boutique was even more special. Lucy had heard rave reviews from clients who had stayed there.

Outside the airport, the warmth of the night air wrapped round her like soft cashmere as the chauffeur opened the doors of a large Mercedes limousine for them.

Marcus slid into the sea next to her and the chauffeur closed the doors.

'Where exactly is Beatrice's villa?' she asked Marcus uncertainly as the Mercedes joined the queue of traffic waiting to leave the airport.

'Up in the hills outside Palma.'

'But that's a long way from Deia,' Lucy objected. 'Wouldn't it have been better for us to have stayed somewhere closer?'

'The Boutique has an excellent reputation, and I thought you'd prefer to stay there.'

'How long will it take us to get there?' Lucy asked.

'Not that long. Why?'

'I need another caffeine fix. I'm desperate for cup of coffee.'

And *he* was desperate for *her*, Marcus found himself thinking. 'Do you want me to ask the driver to stop somewhere?'

Lucy shook her head. 'No, I'll wait.'

She was beginning to feel tired, and more than a little

bit headachy, but despite the comfort of the Mercedes she couldn't relax properly—not with Marcus right there next to her.

The road climbed and turned, winding through the hills, and then started to drop down again. Below them Lucy could see the lights of villas, dotted either side of the river ravine, and below them the small harbour itself. Pure, perfect picture-postcard stuff.

The Mercedes turned in to a narrow stone tunnel beyond which lay a paved forecourt. Within seconds, or so it seemed, they were standing in the jasmine-scented coolness of the foyer, a huge fan whirring above their heads, traditional terracotta tiles underfoot, and the décor echoing the very best of traditional Majorcan interiors. The white walls were warmed by striking paintings and woven rugs in rich earthy colours.

'If you will follow José, he will show you to your suites.' The receptionist smiled as she handed Marcus two key cards, and a very young and very handsome young Majorcan appeared from out of nowhere to assist them.

The lift was tucked away discreetly in a corner, and as it bore them upwards José told them proudly, 'You have the best suites in the whole hotel. The King of Spain himself, he has stayed there with his family.'

The lift stopped and José held the doors open, giving Lucy a small bow as he encouraged her to step through ahead of him.

A short, wide corridor lay in front of her, its walls painted white and hung with more paintings. Lucy was tempted to linger and inspect them more closely, drawn by the richness of the oil paint, but her head was pounding and she was desperate for coffee.

Only two doors opened off the corridor. José stopped at

the first of them and opened the door, inviting Lucy to step inside.

As she did so, her eyes widened in appreciation. In front of her was a large room with a high ceiling, furnished with traditional dark, heavy wooden furniture which included a huge four-poster bed. Floor-to-ceiling wooden shutters filled one wall, and when José went to open them for her Lucy gasped in delight. The shutters concealed glass patio doors beyond which was a well-lit private terrace, complete with its own plunge pool, and beyond that an uninterrupted view of the sea and sky.

'Thank you, José. I'll find my own way around everything.' Lucy smiled and tipped him so that he could leave and show Marcus to his suite.

As soon as she had closed the door behind José, Lucy picked up the telephone and hurriedly dialled Room Service. Only when she had ordered her much-needed coffee did she start to study the suite properly.

A wooden screen that could be folded back separated the bedroom from an integral, sensually luxurious huge round bath, set into the floor right in front of the patio windows so that one might lie in the bath and look out across the terrace and beyond it.

The wall opposite the patio doors was completely mirrored, as was the wall at right angles to it, and set against the right angle was an all-glass shower cubicle, so that in effect one could bathe or shower and see one's reflection in the mirrors at the same time.

She heard a knock on her bedroom door. Her coffee! Wonderful! But when she went to open the door it was Marcus who was standing outside it.

'I've brought you this,' he told her, handing her a card key. 'I'm going to ring Beatrice in a minute, and fix up a meeting with her for tomorrow, but so far as dinner tonight is concerned, there's supposed to be an excellent restaurant down by the harbour. It's eight now, so if I book a table for ten...?'

'Yes. Fine,' Lucy agreed, exhaling in relief as she saw the waiter coming down the corridor.

Ten minutes later, with her caffeine levels replenished, Lucy explored the rest of her suite.

In addition to her open plan bedroom-cum-bathroom, she also had a self-contained dressing room and a second bathroom, with another shower plus bidet and lavatory.

She would have to change before she went out for dinner. A shower would be speedier, but she just couldn't resist the temptation to wallow self-indulgently in the bath.

Lucy lay soaking in the bubble-topped silky warm water of her bath, luxuriating in the sensuality of the experience. She had left her shutters open, so that she could enjoy the view out to sea should she feel energetic enough to lift her head off the bath pillow. Instead, though, she opened her eyes and looked towards the mirrored wall. There was something irresistibly sensual about the combination of a huge bath and a mirror in which one could see oneself using it. This was definitely a suite for lovers.

Lovers. There was only one man she wanted as her lover. Only one man she had ever wanted, full stop. And that man was Marcus.

Marcus.

Was his suite the same as her own? Was he right now lazing in a tub of hot water, his body naked beneath the suds? A shiver of sensual pleasure iced through her own inner heat, as pleasurable as ice-cream melted by hot chocolate sauce—only a thousand times more so.

But she suspected that Marcus was more likely to prefer

a fierce shower to a lazy linger in a bath. And he still hadn't said a word about last night.

Lucy closed her eyes and stroked the soapy water over her skin, imagining that it was still last night and that Marcus was here with her, touching her, stroking her. A wet heat that had nothing at all to do with the water flooded her sex. This was getting dangerous. But she couldn't resist the temptation to lie there and fantasise, to imagine and remember. She closed her eyes...

She had almost fallen asleep in the bath! And look at the time! It was gone nine o'clock. Reaching for the plug, Lucy stepped up out of the bath and reached for one of the deliciously thick, fluffy towels. The mirror threw back her reflection—white soap bubbles slithering silkily down her body, covering her sex and then revealing it. She could feel the hot beat of her own desire as it pulsed out its hungry message. Her fingers touched her own body, stroking the foam from the swell of her mound and then moving lower. She watched her own movements in the mirrors, unable to look away. Her heart had started to race, a fierce wanton urgency filling her. Slowly and delicately, her tongue-tip pressed to her teeth, Lucy ran an experimental finger along her mound and pressed lightly against her clitoris.

Marcus... Immediately her flesh swelled and glistened richly, her heart pumping...

Somewhere outside the intensity of her concentration she heard a noise that sounded like a door opening...

A door opening! Immediately she removed her hand and reached for a towel, her face burning with self-conscious heat as she realised that Marcus was standing in her bedroom.

How long had he been there? How much had he seen? Behind him she could see what must be a connecting door between the two suites. He must have knocked, but she had obviously been too preoccupied to hear him. Her face burned with the knowledge of what she had so nearly been preoccupied with!

'How much longer is it going to take you to get ready?' he asked her. 'Only it's nearly nine-thirty now.'

He, Lucy recognised dizzily, was already changed, wearing a pair of light-coloured chinos with a darker-coloured top.

'I'm virtually there,' she replied, and then blushed vividly as she realised just what connotation could be placed on her comment, and how appropriate it had almost been. She did not dare look at Marcus as she almost scurried past him and into her dressing room.

'It's a long, steep walk down to the harbour, so I've asked the hotel to provide us with a car and a driver,' Marcus announced as they walked into the foyer together, and Lucy glanced down at her strappy-sandal-shod feet. The same sandals she had been wearing yesterday. The same sandals one of which she had left on his stairs, and then found placed neatly with its twin this morning, alongside her clothes...

She wasn't normally a fan of high-heeled shoes, but the dress she was wearing had a pretty handkerchief hem and demanded equally pretty footwear.

From the hotel, the road to the harbour wound down alongside the river, the wooded slopes broken up by the lights of a scattering of expensive luxury villas,

The harbour itself was tiny, and predictably filled with sleek expensive-looking yachts—just as the restaurants fronting onto the harbour were filled with equally sleek and expensive-looking diners.

This was very much Notting-Hill-on-Sea territory, Lucy thought ruefully. Within seconds of leaving their car and taking less than half a dozen steps, she had seen at least half a dozen famous faces amongst the groups of people already seated at the tables set up outside the restaurants and bars.

'The place I've booked us into has a reputation for serving top-quality fish dishes,' Marcus told her. 'And, knowing how much you like fish, I thought you might prefer that to a more traditional tapas bar.'

'Yes, I would,' Lucy agreed, as she stifled a small yawn.

'Sleepy?'

'No, not really. I think my bath must have made me feel tired,' Lucy responded without thinking, and then felt her whole body start to burn as she tensed, dreading hearing Marcus say that he knew exactly why she might be feeling tired.

There was really no reason for her to feel embarrassed about something so natural. Heavens, she didn't know any women of her own age who were not prepared to trade opinions on the latest vibrator. But somehow the fact that Marcus might have seen her almost engaged in such a very intimate and personal act of self-pleasure made her feel acutely embarrassed. Especially after last night. Oh, yes, especially after last night. Now he might think that it was her desire for him that had prompted her to such a course of action.

He might think it, but she actually *knew* it, Lucy admitted to herself, as Marcus guided her between the packed tables and into the restaurant itself.

Typically, Marcus had managed to secure them a table with just about the best view of the harbour possible, and he had been right about the food as well, Lucy saw, when her own meal was placed in front her. Her mouth started to water. Pan-fried scallops with an Asian fusion-style warm salad. Marcus, she noted, had chosen a thick tuna steak.

'More wine?'

Lucy shook her head firmly. She was already on her second glass, and beginning to feel pleasantly relaxed. She didn't need or want any more.

Marcus had only had two glasses himself, although she noticed that, unlike her, he did not nod his head when the waiter asked if they wanted coffee.

'Espresso?' he commented after she had given her order. 'You'll never sleep.'

'Watch me,' Lucy answered flippantly, and then went bright red. Heavens, Marcus was going to think she was propositioning him if she kept on saying idiotic things like that.

Watch her? Oh, he would love to... And not only watch, either.

'What time did you say we were seeing Beatrice tomorrow?' Lucy asked Marcus hastily, trying to sound businesslike and efficient.

'She's going to ring me in the morning to confirm,' Marcus told her as he glanced at his watch. 'I don't want to rush you, but the car should be back for us any minute now.'

Her coffee had arrived and Lucy drank it greedily, relishing both its smell and its taste, while Marcus summoned their waiter and asked for the bill.

She certainly wasn't going to risk having another bath after what had happened earlier, Lucy decided as she locked her suite door and stepped out of her sandals. Instead she would make do with a shower. She yawned sleepily.

After last night, and then Marcus walking in on her and

almost finding her touching herself, she should have been on edge all evening, but instead she had actually felt very relaxed—so relaxed, in fact, that on a couple of occasions she had even laughed. Marcus had proved to be an unexpectedly entertaining and interesting dinner companion, and she had been sorry when the evening had come to an end—and not just because, given the choice, she would have so much preferred to end it in Marcus's arms, in Marcus's bed.

She undressed quickly and pulled on the complimentary bathrobe before tidying away her clothes and heading for the shower.

She had just stepped out of it and towelled herself her dry when she heard a knock on her patio window. She realised that Marcus was standing outside, beckoning to her. Like her, he too was wearing a bathrobe, but whereas on her it fell to the floor and trailed behind her, on Marcus it only just covered his knees. The sight of the bare tanned flesh of his legs made the muscles in her lower body clench in unmistakable need.

Fighting down her reaction, she went to open the door, pulling her own robe protectively around her as she did so. Marcus had obviously walked across from his own suite, she recognised, and she realised that they actually shared the terrace, which ran the full length of both suites.

'Marcus, I was just about to go to bed,' she protested.

He ignored her, taking hold of her arm and commanding, 'Come and look at this,' as he drew her towards the stone parapet that edged the terrace.

'Look at what?' she demanded, and then stood still, a soft 'Oh!' of pleasure escaping from her lips as down below their hotel, at one of the villas, fireworks exploded in a burst of scarlet stars.

'Fireworks,' she whispered, entranced.

'I remembered how much you like them.' Marcus smiled.

'They're magical—like champagne in the sky,' Lucy responded softly. 'Someone must be celebrating something.'

As he wanted to celebrate her, Marcus thought. But in a far more private and intimate way. He would gladly create sexual fireworks for her if she would just allow him.

Another burst of stars followed the first one, this time a shower of sparkling silver and white against the night dark sky.

She looked as excited and enthralled as a small child, Marcus reflected, as she hung onto the stone balustrade and watched. But she wasn't a child.

Lucy could feel Marcus standing behind her, the warmth of his body taking the chill of the evening breeze from hers and making her want to lean back against him...skin to skin...whilst the fireworks lit the sky and her own desire exploded inside her. She looked down. Marcus was leaning forward to get a better view of the fireworks, his hands either side of her own, so that she was enclosed between his body and the parapet.

A burst of gold and crimson exploded into the darkness before falling back to earth...

'Oh, Marcus...' Without thinking, she turned round. He was so close to her. So very close.

'Marcus...' She looked up at his mouth and swallowed. Oh, God, but she wanted him.

'They've finished now. I'd better go in,' she told him jerkily, almost pushing him out of her way in her desperate need to get away from him before she did something even more stupid than she had done already.

She was in so much of a rush that she didn't realise he had followed her inside her suite and was closing the patio door until it was too late.

She couldn't even move when he began to walk towards her, her mouth suddenly too dry for her to speak and her legs too weak for her to move.

In complete silence he took hold of her hand and drew her with him toward the bath and then past it, until they were standing in front of the mirror. Just where she had been standing earlier, when he had...

The colour came and went in her face as he took her in his arms and started to kiss her, holding her face in his hands whilst he brushed her trembling lips over and over again with his own, until she had forgotten everything but her own need to have his mouth on her now, longer and harder. Her own hands rose to cover his shoulders, her fingers digging deep into the muscles as she shuddered fiercely beneath the sudden thrusting possession of his tongue. She felt his hands on her body, pushing the robe off her shoulders, and immediately she dropped her arms so that she could step out of it.

Very slowly Marcus turned her round and drew her back against himself, so that she was facing the mirror and he was standing behind her. His hands skimmed her body, stroking her skin, cupping her breasts, whilst her nipples pushed eagerly against his touch and his mouth teased the sensitive pleasure spot just behind her ear.

Her whole body arched as the breath left her lungs in a sob of erotic longing. Helplessly Lucy closed her eyes— half shocked by the sight of her own naked arousal and the erotic movement of Marcus's hands over her body, and half so aroused by it that she wanted him to take her there and then. To bend her forward until she could rest her hands against the mirror, whilst her hair tumbled round her face and Marcus spread open her thighs, sliding his hands up to her hips whilst he plunged into the female heart of her in a position that was so sensually, shockingly, eternally primitive and immediate.

She was wet, so very wet, and hot and aching, her muscles quivering in anticipation of the pleasure and satisfaction her body craved.

'Open your eyes, Lucy, and look in the mirror.'

Very slowly, she did so.

Marcus caressed her naked shoulders, his hands sliding down to cup her breasts whilst he kissed her throat. The sensation of the slightly rough pads of his fingertips against the exquisite sensitivity of her tight nipples made her cry out and arch her back, to bring her breasts closer to his caress while she pressed her buttocks back against him in eager, urgent movement.

'Is that good?'

His voice sounded thicker, deeper, sending a message to her own senses like a note running along a wire. He was plucking erotically at her nipples, his tanned skin a contrast to her own pale softness and the dark hot flush of her engorged flesh.

His hands moved lower down, over her ribcage, lower... Lucy sighed and squirmed, closing her eyes in anticipation of the pleasure to come.

'No...open your eyes and watch me,' Marcus insisted thickly.

He was stroking her sex. Lucy couldn't remove her aroused gaze from the movement of his hands. Her heart started to hammer against the wall of her chest as slowly and deliberately he folded back the soft flesh—just as she herself had done earlier. She looked into the mirror and saw in his eyes that he had seen her, had known what she was thinking. What she had been wanting. What she had been on the verge of doing....

'Isn't this better?' he demanded softly. 'Why pleasure yourself, Lucy, when I can do it for you?'

His mouth caressed the magic spot just below her ear and her whole body convulsed.

'Did you know that the nerve-endings in this spot here are directly connected to your nerve-endings right here?' she heard him whisper in her ear, as he kissed her skin again and stroked his fingers over the eager, dark pink wetness of her sex, rubbed his thumb-tip slowly over her clitoris.

Once. Twice. And then faster. Until she was breathing frantically fast and her whole body was shuddering in the grip of orgasm.

She couldn't move. She couldn't even stand. She felt boneless, weightless...and pleasured. Pleasured, but not satisfied, she knew, as Marcus swung her up into his arms and carried her over to the bed.

Only when he had placed her on it and removed his own robe, only when her reckless longing had directed her fingers to reach out and stroke the length of his erection and back again, and she had allowed herself to enjoy the delicious pleasure touching him had relayed via her fingertips to each and every one of her senses, did she think to say uncertainly, 'Marcus, I don't think we should be doing this...'

'Why ever not? You enjoyed it last night, didn't you?'

Enjoyed it? Of course she'd enjoyed it. But that wasn't the issue, or the point she was trying to make.

And yet she was murmuring dizzily, 'Oh, yes, I did.'

'And so did I. So there's no problem, is there?'

'No, I don't suppose there is,' Lucy agreed weakly.

How could there be any kind of problem when Marcus was touching her like this? Kissing her like this? 'Mmm,' she sighed happily against his mouth, and she reached up and wrapped her arms tightly around him.

CHAPTER SIX

LUCY looked at the pillow next to her own. It was still squashed from having Marcus's sleeping head lying on it. She reached out and tenderly traced the indentation, a smile of soft happiness curving her mouth. Last night had been so wonderful—and what had made it even more wonderful had been falling asleep cuddled up next to Marcus, free to snuggle in against him and breathe in the scent of him. She had woken up several times during the night, just for the pleasure of reassuring herself that he was still there.

But he wasn't always going to be 'still there', was he? She had no idea what had prompted Marcus to indulge in this brief and unexpected sexual adventure with her, but she knew already how much it was going to hurt when he grew tired of it—and of her. She didn't want Marcus for a brief fling. She wanted him for life. Despair swamped her earlier euphoria.

'Come on, sleepyhead, wake up. I've ordered breakfast, and it will be here any minute.'

Marcus! Lucy shot upright in the bed, and then blushed and reached for the protection of the duvet to cover her bare beasts, all too aware of the amused and quizzical look in Marcus's eyes. He sat down beside her, firmly removed her 'protection', and bent his head to kiss first one nipple and then the other. Then he murmured appreciatively, 'Maybe I should phone Room Service and tell them to delay breakfast.'

'Mmm,' Lucy agreed weakly, and then grabbed for the duvet again when there was a knock on the door.

'I'll get them to take our breakfast through my suite onto the terrace,' Marcus offered, leaving the bed to go and close the shutters for her. 'But don't you dare go back to sleep.'

Sleep! That was the last thing she felt like doing, Lucy thought as she headed for the shower.

'I was just about to come and make sure you hadn't gone back to sleep,' Marcus told her ten minutes later, when she opened the shutters and walked through the patio doors onto the terrace.

'I've ordered coffee for you,' he continued. 'And fruit juice, and poached eggs with tomatoes and mushrooms. There's some toast as well.'

'A cooked breakfast? Yuck.' Lucy shuddered as she sat down and immediately looked longingly at the coffee pot.

Marcus was already pouring coffee for her, and she breathed in its rich aroma whilst her tastebuds prepared themselves for their morning surge of caffeine. Marcus, she noticed, was drinking green tea.

'The body needs protein in the morning,' Marcus told her firmly, as he removed the cover from his own break-fast. 'It can't function properly without it.'

'Oh, thank you, Dr Atkins,' Lucy retorted sourly as she reached for her coffee. But the eggs did look appetising. She reached out and pinched a mushroom from Marcus's plate.

'Eat,' Marcus commanded, handing her her own break-fast. 'As soon as we've finished breakfast I'll go and ring Beatrice and check what time she's expecting to meet up with us,' he added, as she tucked into her eggs and realised just how hungry she actually was. 'But first there is some-thing I want to discuss with you.'

Lucy had to put down her coffee cup because her hand

had started to tremble. Here it was—the demand for an explanation she had been dreading so much.

'If it's about last night...and...and the day before...' she began defensively.

'It is,' Marcus agreed. 'It seems to me, Lucy, that it would be a very good idea if you and I were to get married.'

Had she head him correctly? Was he trying to make some kind of joke? 'Married? You mean, as in to one another?' she asked him cautiously.

'Of course I mean as in to one another.'

'But—but, Marcus...why? I mean, why would you—we—want to do that? I mean, you don't even like me very much!' Lucy blurted out, too shocked not to be honest.

'I think that you and I would be very well suited to one another.'

Lucy reached for her coffee cup and took a deep gulp. He hadn't said that he did like her, she noticed. And he certainly hadn't said that he loved her.

'We share a similar background, and I suspect a very similar outlook on life. We both, I think, want children, and, despite the ending of your marriage to Nick, I believe that, like me, you think of commitment made to another person via marriage as one that is made for life—for better or for worse, in a relationship to which one is totally committed. Because make no mistake—if we do marry, I shall be committed completely and totally to our marriage, and to you and to our children, and I shall expect the same commitment from you.'

Total and complete commitment from Marcus to her? Was she dreaming?

'But—but...'

'But what?' Marcus demanded coolly. 'As the last two

days have proved, we are exceptionally sexually compatible.'

'But people don't get married just because they are having good sex together!' Lucy protested. 'You can't want to marry me because of that, Marcus.'

'There are other reasons,' he agreed.

'What other reasons?'

'I'll be thirty-five in December,' Marcus told her calmly. 'All the men in my family—my father, my grandfather, my great-grandfather and back beyond that—married before they were thirty-five. It's a family tradition, and one I have no intention of breaking.'

Did he mean that if she refused him he would find someone else who wouldn't?

She thought about how it would feel, being married to Marcus without being loved by him when she loved him so much. It would hurt—and very badly. Then she thought about how she would feel seeing Marcus married to someone else because he wanted to be married before his thirty-fifth birthday.

There just wasn't any comparison. She could not bear the thought of seeing Marcus married to someone else when she could have been married to him herself.

'And we have to be aware of the fact that, since you don't take the pill and I haven't been using any form of contraception, you might already have conceived my child,' Marcus reminded her. 'I know how much you love children, Lucy, but I don't think you'd want to be a single mother—and I certainly wouldn't allow you to bring up my child without me being a part of its life. It would be far more practical for us to get married.'

Practical! She didn't want practical. She wanted undying love, and promises that she would be showered with kisses day and night.

But Marcus didn't love her, Lucy reminded herself sternly. Just as Nick hadn't loved her—and look what had happened there.

She couldn't marry him. And she couldn't *not* marry him.

She hadn't loved Nick, had she? But she did love Marcus—and besides, Marcus was a completely different man from Nick. Marcus had stated unequivocally that their marriage would be a permanent commitment, and that meant it would be exactly that. And she wanted that. She wanted it so very badly. She wanted to wake up every morning in a bed she shared with him, she wanted to conceive his children, and she wanted to grow old with him.

Love could grow, couldn't it? And Marcus did want her. Unlike Nick, Marcus wanted to have sex with her. Unlike Nick, Marcus enjoyed having sex with her—he had said so.

'Marcus, *if* we were to...to become a couple, don't you think that people might think it rather odd and ask questions?'

'Why should they? And if they do I shall simply tell them that I had always planned to marry you, and that since Blayne beat me to it first time round I'm making sure I don't lose you to anyone else.'

Tears stung the backs of her eyes. If only that was the truth.

'So, are you willing to accept my proposal? I promise you that I think a marriage between us will work very well, Lucy, and I shall certainly do everything within my power to ensure that it does.'

'I don't know. I'm so confused...'

Marcus sounded more as though he were chairing a business meeting than proposing to her. But then to him no doubt their marriage *was* a kind of business arrangement, she thought sadly.

'Perhaps I should take you back to bed,' Marcus murmured softly. 'That might help make up your mind.'

Her insides melted, then somehow she was nodding her head, and Marcus was saying coolly, 'Good, so it's agreed, then. We won't say anything official until I've had a chance to speak to your father—and besides, I'd prefer us to wait until we return to London to choose your ring. There is a family betrothal ring—so astoundingly ugly, according to my mother, that she threatened not to marry my father unless he allowed her to choose something for herself—but personally, I think that for an engaged couple to opt for a ring of their own choosing invests it with something more personal and shared than the passing-down of a family ring—'

'I agree with you.' Lucy stopped him dizzily. Was this really happening? Was she really sitting here over breakfast with Marcus, talking about their marriage and her engagement ring, having just spent a wonderful night in bed with him?

'We're virtually in October now,' Marcus continued. 'My birthday is in early December, so I'd like to be married before the end of November if possible. Just a small affair—if that's all right with you?'

'Oh, yes. Of course. A simple register office ceremony...'

'No.' Marcus shook his head, silencing her. 'No, I'd prefer a church service, Lucy. After all, I think we're both agreed that we are making a lifetime commitment to one another—I certainly view our marriage as a permanent commitment. Since you and Blayne didn't marry in church, there is, in my opinion, no moral or legal reason why we should not do so. And even if the actual wedding has to be in a register office I'd like a church blessing, if possible. I imagine the Brompton Oratory would be the best choice. You'll want to be married from your parents' London home, and since that is in Knightsbridge...'

Lucy stared at him. The Oratory was *the* church of choice for lots of society brides and their mothers, and very grand.

Marcus was looking at his watch.

'It's nearly eleven now, and we're meeting Beatrice at twelve-thirty in Palma to have lunch with her. So that only leaves us half an hour to get ready—besides which, I'd better give her a ring and remind her. She's got possibly the worst memory of anyone I know.'

They both stood up, and then on some impulse she didn't want to investigate too closely Lucy put her hand on Marcus's arm and tugged at the sleeve of his robe, so that he bent his head towards her. Raising herself up on her tiptoes, she pressed her mouth to his and kissed him softly.

She could feel the rigidity of his muscles, and her face burned as she released him and stepped back from him.

Marcus watched her through narrowed eyes. It was one thing for her to want him, but he wasn't sure how he felt about the intensity with which he wanted her back. It would suit his purposes very nicely for her to lose control in his arms, but he certainly did not want his own self-control to be breached—and he didn't like having to admit that it could be—especially not by Lucy.

Even so, he couldn't afford to risk alienating her at this stage by appearing to reject her.

Lucy exhaled in shock as Marcus reached for her and drew her back into his arms.

How and when had Marcus's hands slipped inside her robe to her naked skin? she wondered blissfully, when she suddenly realised that the sensation of his mouth on hers wasn't the only sensual pleasure she was experiencing.

Instinctively she moved closer to him, and discovered to her delight that he was aroused and hard. She made a small sound of female pleasure and approval as she pressed even closer—and then reluctantly she remembered Beatrice.

'You said we should get ready to meet your sister,' she reminded him, the words semi-mumbled beneath the increasing passion of his kiss.

'To hell with Beatrice,' she heard him respond thickly, but he started to release her, giving her one last hard kiss as he did so, acknowledging, 'Yes, you're right. We'd better make a move.'

She was going to marry Marcus. She still couldn't take it in.

They had arrived in Palma five minutes earlier, having been driven there by the hotel's chauffeur service.

'I thought we'd be going to Beatrice's villa to discuss the party,' Lucy commented.

'Beatrice suggested we meet up for lunch instead,' Marcus answered. 'The restaurant's just down here.'

Lucy knew Palma quite well, and the restaurant in front of them was one that was patronised by wealthy locals and visitors alike. Knowing how elegantly and expensively Marcus's elder sister dressed, Lucy had decided to wear something a little bit more formal than she would normally have chosen—and now that she had seen where they were to have lunch she was glad of that fact. Her linen skirt with its row of pretty eyelet details just above the hem, teamed with a white strappy top worn under a crunchy cotton-linen asymmetrically styled cardigan-type jacket, had been a good choice; virtually every other woman in the restaurant seemed to be wearing a combination of very stylish linens and cottons, in that smart way that continental women seemed to be able to adopt so easily.

'Beatrice obviously hasn't arrived yet, but we may as well go straight to our table and wait for her there—unless you want a drink in the bar first?' Marcus suggested.

'No, let's go straight to the table,' Lucy told him. She didn't want him thinking that she couldn't get through half a day without an alcoholic drink, especially when it wasn't true. Coffee, now—well, that was different.

They had been waiting for about five minutes when the restaurant door opened and Marcus's sister came hurrying in. Tall and dark-haired, like Marcus, she was wearing black linen pants and an oatmeal-coloured cotton top, her hair drawn back off her face, her large Oliver's People sunglasses perched on top of her head.

'Marcus!' she exclaimed as she hurried over and kissed him. 'I am so sorry I'm late. And Lucy—how very kind of you to give up your time like this.'

'We haven't ordered anything yet, Bea. Would you like something to drink?' Marcus asked, as the waiter drew out her chair for her.

'Oh, yes—a spritzer, please. I'm driving. That's why I was late. I couldn't find anywhere to park. What's the weather like at home? When I spoke to Mother the other day she said it was raining. I'm going to have to stay out here until half term, and the wretched plumber says now that he can't get the tiles we ordered, which means that when Boffy and Izzy come out for their half term break we'll only have one bathroom.'

Lucy already knew that—contrary to her rather formidable appearance—Beatrice was something of a 'dizzy brunette', but it still bemused her to hear Beatrice expressing such sentiments when the only reason Lucy was here was so that they could talk about George's surprise birthday party without him knowing.

'I can definitely recommend the food here, Lucy,' Beatrice told her. 'Especially the fish. Although perhaps not the bouillabaisse—it is rather an acquired taste.'

The menus arrived, and while Marcus and Beatrice talked, or rather Beatrice talked and Marcus listened, Lucy studied hers.

'Have you had any thoughts about George's party, Beatrice?' Lucy asked, once the waiter had taken their orders.

'What? Oh, not really. George wants something small—just a few family and friends. He has this thing about castles, and he did wonder if we might hire one somewhere. What do you think?'

'Well, that's certainly possible,' Lucy agreed, mentally rolling her eyes.

Their food had arrived, and Lucy eyed her plate hungrily. It must be all the sex she was having that was giving her such a good appetite, she decided, and then went bright red as the thought of sex and appetite somehow led to thoughts of those two elements combined together, and all the ways that Marcus might satisfy her hunger for him.

'Goodness, Lucy, you look quite flushed. Are you all right? It is warm in here. I think we can talk more about George's party once I'm back in London. After all, I've got until next year, and right now these wretched workmen have got me in such a state I can't think about anything else.'

They had all finished eating, and Marcus turned to Lucy and asked calmly, 'What about pudding?'

'Not for me. But I would love an espresso.'

'An espresso? Lucy, my dear, is that wise? All that caffeine in your system will have you chattering non-stop for the rest of the day.'

Lucy had to bite the inside of her cheek to stop herself from giggling, and then she made the mistake of looking at Marcus. He looked every bit as amused as she felt, and when he gave her a small, rueful and very private smile Lucy felt as though she had been handed the keys to heaven. She and Marcus were sharing an intimate moment of understanding and humour, just as though they were really in a *proper* relationship.

Suddenly Lucy felt as though she could touch the sky and reach for anything—even one day, perhaps, Marcus's love.

'I can't wait to ring Mother and tell her that I've seen you both,' Beatrice announced twenty minutes later, after they had walked her back to her car. She then not only hugged Lucy but also kissed her affectionately as well, before saying meaningfully, 'Mother is going to be so pleased. She's always had a soft spot for Lucy...'

'Marcus, I think Beatrice has guessed about us,' Lucy warned him after they had waved goodbye to her.

'I should hope so, after all the hints I dropped,' Marcus agreed dryly.

'What? You said we weren't going to tell anyone yet!'

'I haven't told her. I've just dropped a few hints. Knowing Beatrice the way I do, it won't be very long before she's convinced herself that she guessed about us ages ago—and that should help to ease away any uncomfortable questions about the speed with which things have happened.'

It would also place another barrier in the way of Lucy changing her mind and backing out of marrying him, Marcus reflected cynically.

'We've got another hour before the hotel chauffeur is due to pick us up. How about a walk?'

'Lovely,' Lucy told him, and meant it.

What she hadn't been prepared for was that Marcus would choose to walk in the direction of a very expensive-looking jewellers and then draw her towards its windows. 'See anything you like?' he asked.

'I thought you said we wouldn't get a ring until we get home?'

'Yes, of course—for one thing I thought you might want to choose a stone and then a setting—but I wasn't thinking of a ring right now, Lucy. You've just agreed to be my wife, and, whilst your engagement ring will be a public acknowledgement of that fact, I would like to celebrate it with something rather more personal—a pair of earrings, perhaps? Something like those?' he added, indicating the very pair of diamond studs Lucy hadn't been able to stop gazing at.

'Marcus, you don't have to buy me anything,' she protested.

'That's right. I don't have to,' he agreed blandly as he rang the bell for admittance to the shop. 'But I do want to.'

They were inside the shop—all thick carpets, glass display cases, the quiet and very serious hum of air-conditioning and wealth, and immaculately groomed young male and female sales assistants.

As soon as Marcus told one of them what he wanted, they were taken to a small private room and offered comfortable seats.

'Perhaps you would care for a drink—water, coffee?' the sales assistant offered.

'Oh, coffee please.' Lucy thanked him, ignoring the way Marcus lifted his eyebrow. 'Okay, so you don't do caffeine,' she hissed, as soon as they were alone. 'But I do.'

'Caffeine and champagne,' Marcus agreed dryly.

The salesman was returning, carrying Lucy's coffee and accompanied by an older, obviously more senior member of the shop's staff. It was too late for Lucy to defend herself on the champagne charge.

'You have an excellent eye if I may say so, *señora*,' the senior salesman told Lucy approvingly as he spread the roll of fabric he was carrying on top of the immaculate glass and then placed the earrings on it.

'These stones are excellent quality, and without any blemish. They are D quality, which means they have exceptional clarity and purity. They are one and a half carats each, and set in platinum.'

And they would cost a fortune, Lucy recognised, as she mentally said goodbye to them.

'They are lovely,' she began 'But—'

'Why don't you try them on?' Marcus overrode her.

Reluctantly, Lucy did so, and then looked at her reflection in the mirror the salesman gave her. The stones burned with blue-white fire and were, as he had said, of exceptional purity.

'Please excuse me a moment,' the salesman murmured, getting up and leaving the room.

'Marcus, you mustn't buy me these,' Lucy told him as soon as they were alone.

'Why not? Don't you like them? Personally, I think they suit you very well.'

Not like them? Was he kidding? No woman could possibly not like diamonds such as these.

'Of course I like them. But that isn't the point.'

'No? Then what is?' he challenged her.

'The cost, of course. Marcus, these are going to be dreadfully expensive.' She looked so worried, with her forehead creased in that small frown and her eyes shadowed with anxiety, that it actually made him frown himself. She was the first woman he had ever bought jewellery for who had begged him not to do so because of its cost.

The salesman had returned, carrying a small square box.

'We'll take the earrings. My fiancée loves them,' Marcus announced coolly.

The salesman beamed. 'Ah, *señor*, you will not regret their purchase, I do assure you. They will more than keep their value. And it occurs to me that you might like to see this bangle, which has the same quality of stones, but of only one carat each. The bangle itself is made of platinum and white gold. The design is modern but delicate,' he enthused, removing the bangle from its box so that they could see it.

Once again Lucy found that she was holding her breath. The bangle was beautiful, simple and elegant, its simple curving lines set with three diamonds all offset from one another.

'Try it on,' Marcus urged her.

Lucy shook her head. 'No,' she told him firmly, standing up with a determination that rather astonished her. 'It is beautiful,' she agreed, turning to the salesman. 'But I don't wear very much jewellery, other than my watch. The earrings are more than enough.'

Lucy waited discreetly in the main part of the shop whilst Marcus paid for her earrings, then automatically fell into step beside him as they walked back outside into the late-afternoon sunshine. She longed to move closer to him, to slip her arm through his, or even better for him to take her hand in his. But of course he did no such thing. A small, unexpectedly sharp pang of pain seized her.

'Thank you for my earrings, Marcus,' she told him quietly, fighting back her longing to turn towards him and kiss him. 'They are beautiful, but really you shouldn't have.'

She watched as he gave a dismissive, almost uncaring shrug. 'Of course I should. Is there anything else you'd like to look at? Only our car should be here in another few minutes.'

Lucy shook her head. If she was honest, what she wanted to do right now, more than anything else, was to go back to their hotel so that she could be on her own with Marcus.

The ache that had begun earlier in her bedroom, when he had kissed her, had gradually but very determinedly been increasing in intensity all the time she had been with him, and it was now an urgent pulsing female need that was overriding any other desire she might have had. She wanted Marcus and she wanted him desperately, eagerly, completely and utterly. And, what was more, that wanting had nothing whatsoever to do with the diamonds or anything else he might buy her.

'How do you feel about having dinner here on the terrace this evening? We can go out, if you like, or dine in the hotel restaurant. But I thought in view of the fact that we shall be returning to London tomorrow morning, in our new role as an engaged couple, this evening might be a good opportunity to discuss any concerns you might have about the future.'

'Dinner on the terrace sounds wonderful,' Lucy told Marcus truthfully. They were in her suite, having just returned from Palma.

'We're going to have to talk about Prêt a Party, and how you visualise its future at some stage,' Marcus continued.

Prêt a Party! Lucy realised with shock that she had barely given her business a thought since she had Marcus had stepped onto their flight to Palma.

'Oh, you don't—' She began immediately to reassure Marcus that he did not need to worry that she would be expecting him to rescue her ailing business from debt, and then stopped. Andrew Walker had said that he didn't want her to mention their discussion to anyone at this stage, and until he actually came back to her with a firm offer there wasn't really anything to discuss, was there? If she told Marcus now that her problems with her business were over, that Prêt a Party had a potential investor, and then had to tell him that she had been let down, she was going to look very silly and gullible. Just as she had done when Nick had cheated her. She could still remember how angry and contemptuous Marcus had been then. She didn't want that to happen a second time.

'Must we talk about Prêt a Party tonight?' Lucy asked him. 'Only...'

'Only what?' Marcus probed.

'Only I thought that tonight could be for...us,' Lucy whispered, pink-cheeked. She could feel her blush deepening as she saw the way he was looking at her.

'For us? Well, it certainly might be a good idea if we discuss some of the practical issues we need to sort out.'

Disappointment filled her. That was not what she had meant at all.

'Practical issues?' Did he mean things like contraception? Lucy wondered uncertainly. If so, she would have to find the words to tell him that she relished the experience of feeling him inside her without anything between them so much that she would prefer it if she made herself responsible for that side of things and took the contraceptive pill.

'Yes. Practical issues,' Marcus repeated. 'Such as where we are going to live. I'd prefer to keep my Wendover

Square house as our London home. After all, it's been in my family for nearly two hundred years.'

'It is a lovely house,' Lucy agreed, 'especially with the garden. But I'll want to redecorate it. And I'll definitely want an espresso-maker in the kitchen,' she added teasingly.

'The decorating I do not have a problem with,' Marcus returned dryly. 'The espresso machine might require some in-depth discussion and a compromise. Perhaps even some compensation. But I like the idea of us looking for a house in the country,' he continued.

'Mmm, I'd like that too. Though I'll want to continue to work, Marcus.'

'Of course. So shall I,' he agreed drolly, before looking at his watch and telling her, 'But remember, since we have been having sex without contraception, you could already be pregnant. Running a business and caring for a new baby wouldn't be easy. Look, it's six o'clock now and I need a shower. Why don't I go to my own suite, order dinner for eight, have a shower, get changed, make a couple of phone calls and then meet you outside on the terrace at, say, seven-thirty?'

'Perfect,' Lucy told him, although she was disappointed when he walked over to the communicating door, opened it and walked through it without kissing her before he left.

She would have a shower herself, she decided. Then a small smile curled her mouth as she glanced towards the bath. The thought of enjoying a long lazy soak was very tempting, especially with her memories of the erotic pleasure it had led to later.

She hadn't brought any 'occasion'-type clothes with her, which was another reason to prefer having dinner on their own terrace.

She reached for the telephone and pressed the numbers

for Room Service, so that she could order some coffee, then closed the shutters and pulled out the folding door that enabled her to close off the shower and bathroom area from the rest of the bedroom. Being surprised in the bath by Marcus was one thing; having one of the waiters walk in whilst she was in the shower was something else again—and something that she most definitely did not want to happen.

It didn't take her long to shower. She loved the luxury of thick, fluffy and constantly replenished hotel towels and bathrobes, she reflected, as she dried herself and then smoothed her body with delicious-smelling lotion before pulling on her robe and folding back the sliding doors.

Her coffee had arrived, and she went over to the occasional table to pour it, pausing with a small frown when she saw the dark green, gold-embossed gift-wrapped box lying on the table next to the coffee tray, beside the complimentary hand-made chocolates provided by the hotel. She recognised the name embossed on the ribbon immediately. It was the name of the jewellers they had been in that afternoon.

This hadn't been provided by the hotel, Lucy reflected, as she picked up the box and started to unwrap it. And it was too large to contain her earrings. Her suspicions turned to certainty when she removed the wrapping paper and opened it to find inside the bangle they had been shown in the shop.

Marcus had bought it for her? As well as the earrings? He really was spoiling her. Materially, yes, he was spoiling her. But she would much rather have been spoiled by his love.

In the end they decided that they might as well stay in their robes for dinner. There was no one to see them, after all, and besides, it added a special intimacy to their evening. Lucy looked down at the bangle she was now wearing. The full moon was bathing the terrace in its cool sharp light. Lucy picked up one of her prawns and dipped it in mayonnaise, licking her fingers after she had finished eating it, and then smiling.

'What's the smile for?' Marcus asked.

'I was just thinking about that scene in Henry Fielding's *Tom Jones*—you know, the sex and food one...'

'Oh, yes? Is that a hint?'

Lucy shook her head. 'Certainly not,' she retorted self-consciously, but when he stood up and started to walk very purposefully towards her, her heart did a backflip in giddy excitement and anticipation.

But when he stopped in front of her it wasn't to take her in his arms, as she had been hoping. Instead he produced the small box that contained her earrings.

'I should have given you these.'

He sounded so abrupt and cold that Lucy frowned. He might have said that he wanted to marry her, but he certainly wasn't behaving as though he did.

'You shouldn't have got me this as well,' she told him, touching her bangle. 'The earrings are more than enough.' As she spoke she reached for the box, but to her surprise Marcus shook his head and reached for her hand, pulling her firmly to her feet.

She had to hold her breath as he carefully inserted the earrings into her earlobes. Not because she was afraid he might be too rough, but because she was afraid that she might betray to him just how she felt about him. The sensation of his warm breath on her bare skin was so sensuously erotic that it made her whole body melt with longing for him. She knew that she was trembling inside with the intensity of her feelings, and that very soon she would be trembling outwardly as well.

The earrings were in place, and, had he loved her, this surely should have been the moment when Marcus bent his head and kissed her—a truly special and intimate moment they would both remember for ever—but instead he was moving away from her.

And then, so suddenly, so shockingly that her whole body thrilled erotically, he came back to her, pushing the robe off her shoulders with hard knowing hands that kept her arms straight so that it could fall away completely, while he kissed her so fiercely that she could feel the heavy, erratic thud of his heartbeat as though it were throbbing inside her own chest.

The only sound to break the silence was the acceleration of their combined breathing, and then, as abruptly as he had taken hold of her, Marcus released her mouth and began to caress her eagerly responsive flesh.

Moonlight celebrated the beauty of her naked body. The terrace was private enough for Lucy to know that they could not be overlooked, and there was something gloriously erotic and exciting about standing naked in the moonlight as Marcus caressed her skin with delicate fingertips, brushing his lips against her throat.

'You're wet,' Marcus murmured thickly as his fingers dipped into her sex.

'You made me like that,' Lucy answered him shakily. After all, it was true.

Marcus looked at the night-dark peaks of her nipples and then bent his head to suckle erotically on one of them, whilst his fingers stroked deeper and more firmly. Still caressing her, he arched Lucy back against his arm so that her whole body was offered up to him.

He could feel her moving urgently against him as her desire quickened.

'Marcus,' Lucy moaned, 'I think I'm going to come...'

'Good,' he told her thickly, as he lifted his mouth from her breast to her lips. 'I want you to.'

'I want you inside me,' Lucy begged.

'Later. Don't talk now,' he told her. 'Just enjoy.'

Don't talk. Lucy closed her eyes and gasped as her body tightened and pleasure began to shudder through her.

CHAPTER SEVEN

'MARCUS, are you sure we're doing the right thing?'

They had just returned from visiting her parents, who were overjoyed about the fact that they were to marry, and yet despite the delight with which everyone had greeted the news of their engagement, since they had returned to London Lucy had begun to be gripped by an increasingly intense feeling of sadness and foreboding.

Her vision was clouded with emotional tears as the October sunshine shone in through the windows of the pretty breakfast room overlooking Marcus's garden and bounced off the facets of her engagement ring. She had fallen in love with the simple rectangular diamond with its emerald cut facets the moment she had seen it, and when Marcus had picked it up and said quietly, 'I rather like this one, but of course it must be your choice,' she had been so thrilled she had almost cried with happiness. She had been happy—then!

In Majorca, swept away on a tide of sex and fantasy, she had felt as though anything was possible—even Marcus coming to love her—but now, back in London, certain realities were refusing to go away.

'What exactly do you mean?' Marcus demanded. He was frowning at her with that familiar blend of impatience and irritation that always cramped her stomach and squeezed her heart with pain. 'I should have thought from the response we've had from our families to the news of our impending marriage that it is obvious that we are very much doing the right thing.' He stood up and strode to the window, and Lucy gripped her mug of coffee with tense fingers. It was clear that he didn't want to continue the discussion, but she needed to. She needed... She needed his love, she admitted helplessly. And in the absence of that she needed some kind of acknowledgement of her own fears, and his reassurance that there was nothing for her to fear. She needed hope, and the belief that he could grow to love her. But she couldn't tell him any of those things, she admitted painfully, because she knew that he wouldn't understand her needs and that he would be irritated by them.

'Our families assume that...that we care about one another,' she told him carefully instead. 'They don't know the truth. And I don't know if a...a relationship—a marriage—without love can survive.'

'Love?' Marcus shook his head, his expression darkening. 'Why is everyone so obsessed by this delusion that what they call love is something of any value? It isn't,' he told her harshly. 'You should know that. After all, you married Blayne because you *loved* him, and look where that got you.

'You and I have the kind of practical reasons for marrying one another that are far more important than love. I need and want a wife who understands my way of life and who shares my desire for children—I certainly do not want to be the first Carring not to produce an heir or heiress. Sexually, as we have both already shown, we are compatible. You want children, and you are not the kind of woman who would want them outside a committed relationship. You married once for so-called love, Lucy. I should have thought you were intelligent enough to recognise that that was a mistake, and not want to repeat it.'

'But what if one day you fall in love with someone else, Marcus?'

'Fall in love?' He looked at her as though she had suggested he murder his own mother. 'Haven't you listened to anything I've been saying? So far as I am concerned sexual love is merely a cloak to cover juvenile and selfish—self-obsessed!—emotional folly, allied to lust. My father fell in love, or so he claimed, when he left my mother. He abandoned her and us because of that *love*, and if it hadn't been for the accident that killed him he would have destroyed the bank as well as my mother's happiness. I saw then what *love* was, and I swore that I would never ever allow myself to indulge in such a thing.'

But you were six years old! Lucy wanted to protest. But wisely she refrained from doing so. She had had no idea that Marcus held such strong and bitter views about love, or that he was so antagonistic toward it.

Her coffee had gone cold, but she still kept her hands wrapped around her mug, as though she was trying to seek warmth and comfort from it.

'What is it?' he demanded when he looked at her and saw the despair in her eyes.

She shook her head. 'I...I'm not sure we should get married, Marcus.'

'It's too late for second thoughts now,' he told her sharply. 'For one thing your mother is busily planning the wedding, and for another...' He paused and then reminded her, 'Let's not forget that you could already be carrying my child. We are getting married, Lucy,' he reinforced calmly. 'And nothing is going to change that.'

Just as nothing was going to change the way he felt about love, or his antagonism towards it, Lucy recognised with despair. How could she have deceived herself into believing that he would grow to love her? Marcus would never love her. Marcus didn't want to love her. He didn't want to love anyone.

'I want to talk to you about Prêt a Party,' he continued briskly.

Lucy tensed. She didn't want to talk to Marcus about her business. She had had a letter from Andrew Walker, reiterating that he didn't want her to discuss their meeting with anyone and explaining that he was still out of the country on business and would be in touch with her on his return. Of course there should be no secrets between husband and wife, but she had given her word and she had no intention of breaking it—and besides...Nick's betrayal of her trust had left a painful scar. She knew that Marcus would never cheat her financially, but her growing insecurity about the future of their marriage made her want to hold on tightly to the security of Prêt a Party. If at some future date Marcus chose to decide that their marriage wasn't working with the clockwork efficiency that he had decided that it should, she might need her business—not just to support herself financially, but to validate her as a person.

'I've decided that the simplest way to deal with the current situation would be for me to inject enough capital into the business to clear its debts,' he said.

'No! No—I don't want you to do that.'

Lucy could see that her outburst had surprised him.

'Why not? Less than two months ago you begged me to let you utilise what was left of your trust fund to put into the company.'

'That was different,' she told him stubbornly. 'That was my money, not yours. And besides...' She bit her lip. She couldn't tell him about Andrew Walker—not yet—and even if she did she suspected that he would not understand why she felt able to accept both financial assistance and financial involvement from someone else, but not from him. Having one husband involved in her business and virtually destroying it, and her, had taught her a harsh lesson. It wasn't one she wanted to repeat.

Marcus frowned as he looked at her. It was obvious to him that Lucy was having second thoughts about their marriage. Was it because, despite all that he had done to her, she still loved Nick Blayne? And why was she rejecting his offer to pay off Prêt a Party's debts?

'Lucy...'

She stopped him fiercely. 'Prêt a Party is my responsibility, Marcus, and I want to keep it that way.'

Her responsibility and her salvation, perhaps, should he ever decide to end their marriage.

A feeling of intense inner aloneness filled her. Sometimes it seemed as though her whole emotional life involved keeping painful secrets she could not share with anyone else. She badly wanted to cry, but of course she must not do so. Her two best friends had been so lucky, finding men who were their soul mates and true partners— men with whom they could share every part of their lives and themselves, from their most mundane thoughts to those that were most sacred and private to them. But not her. She never had and now would never be able to share her innermost longings and feelings with anyone.

She gave a small shiver. Marriage to Marcus would mean closing the door on the deepest of her feelings and shutting them away for ever. But she knew she simply wasn't strong enough to let him walk away from her and find someone else. The pain would simply be too much for her to bear. And, as Marcus himself kept reminding her, it could already be too late for her to back out of their coming marriage. She might already have conceived.

Lucy looked at her watch. Marcus would be in Edinburgh by now. He had said that he would only be away for a couple of days, but already she was missing him.

Tonight was the launch of the new football boot—the last of Prêt a Party's major events. She was pleased with the response she had received to the invitations she had sent out, and even Dorland was going to be there. Although corporate events, no matter how lavish, were not really his style.

Her mobile rang, jerking her out of her thoughts, and her heart leapt when she saw that it was Marcus who was calling.

Although she wasn't officially living with him yet, she was spending more nights in Marcus's bed than she was her own.

'Has your mother sent out the wedding invitations yet?' he asked.

'They went out yesterday,' Lucy told him. Her mother had spent several afternoons cloistered in the Holy Grail of stationery requisites that was the basement of Smythson's Sloane Street premises, poring over samples of wedding stationery. 'Although she's telephoned people as well, in view of the lack of time. You do realise just how many guests are going to be at our wedding, don't you, Marcus?' she cautioned him.

'Two hundred and rising at the last count—and that isn't including my second cousins four times removed from Nova Scotia—at least according to my mother and Beatrice,' he relied promptly.

'What? No, Marcus.' Lucy panicked. 'It's more like—'

'Two hundred *each*. That is to say, *my* mother is planning on inviting two hundred guests, whilst I understand *your* mother can't get her list down under two hundred and fifty.'

'Oh, Marcus,' Lucy wailed. 'We said we wanted a quiet wedding.'

'Talk to your mother—apparently that *is* a quiet wedding,' Marcus told her dryly.

Lucy sighed. 'Thank goodness it isn't summer. Ma said the other night that if it had been she thought it would have been a good idea to tent over the gardens in your square.'

'Yes, I've seen it done.'

'So have I, and I know exactly what hard work it is. Anyway, I thought we both agreed that we just want a simple wedding breakfast, somewhere like the Lanesborough—not five hundred people and a ballroom at the Ritz.'

'Well, maybe *we* do, but we aren't our mothers. Stop worrying about it,' Marcus advised her, 'and let them get on with it and enjoy themselves. I don't want you too worn out to enjoy our honeymoon.'

Lucy could feel her face stating to burn.

'If I am, that won't be because of the wedding preparations,' she told him valiantly.

'Shagged out already?' Marcus asked her directly.

'Totally,' Lucy agreed lightly. There was no point in wishing he had spoken more lovingly. 'When will you be back?'

'Oh, not so shagged out that you don't want more?'

'I was asking because of the christening,' Lucy told him in a dignified voice.

'Uh-huh? Well, don't worry, I haven't forgotten that we're driving down to the christening on Thursday.'

Julia and Silas were having their three-month-old son christened at the weekend, and Lucy had been asked to be one of his godmothers along with Carly, the third member of their trio.

Although Silas was based in New York, he and Julia

spent as much time as they could in England, mainly because of Julia's elderly grandfather, and the christening was being held in a small village close to his stately home.

'I'd better go; take care of yourself,' Marcus told her calmly, before ending the call.

No *I love you*; no *do you love me...* But then, how could there be? Marcus didn't love her.

'I'm going now, Mrs Crabtree,' Lucy called out to the housekeeper, forcing back the threatening tears clogging her throat.

Marcus's housekeeper had made it plain that she welcomed the idea of Marcus being married, and she and Lucy had spent several very happy afternoons discussing how best to renovate the slightly old-fashioned kitchen.

'There's a parcel just arrived for you, Lucy,' she called back.

'Oh?' Lucy hurried into the kitchen and stared at the large box sitting on the table.

There was a note attached to it, in Marcus's handwriting.

Hope that this will make our mornings together worth waking up to.

Slightly pink-cheeked, Lucy started to open it. Marcus had already ensured that she thought he was worth waking up to, and it was difficult to imagine how he could make their mornings any more of a sexual pleasure than they already were.

But she realised that had been wrong as she opened the box to reveal not some *outré* sexual toy, but an espresso coffee machine.

'Oh, Marcus!' she whispered, suddenly overwhelmed by the emotions she had been trying to suppress.

'He said as how you were missing your espresso in the morning,' Mrs Crabtree told Lucy with a wide smile.

She desperately wanted to ring him and thank him, but she contented herself instead with simply texting him—in case he was already with his client.

Lucy exhaled slowly in relief. It looked very much as though the evening was going to be the success her corporate clients had hoped for. Having half a dozen Premier League football stars here had certainly been a good draw, and the models and It Girls clustered around them were making heavy inroads into the orange and red striped cocktail invented to match the orange and red flash on the new football boots being promoted.

If so far as the female guests were concerned the footballers were the main attraction, then her clients were equally delighted by the number of media people attending, and had told her so.

The cheerleaders had done their bit and been wildly applauded, and even her tongue-in-cheek curry and chips mini-suppers had been greeted with enthusiasm—especially by the footballers.

'Lucy!'

'Dorland.' Lucy smiled affectionately as the magazine owner and editor took hold of her arm and guided her to one of the tables.

'You're a very naughty girl not telling me about you and Marcus,' he told her, wagging his finger in front of her. 'I had to read about your engagement in *The Times*.'

Lucy gave what she hoped was a convincing laugh. 'Blame Marcus for that, Dorland, not me. But you are coming to the wedding, aren't you?'

His expression softened. 'Of course.'

Lucy had insisted that Dorland was to be invited as a guest, even though her mother had not totally approved.

'Lovely stiffie by the way, sweetie. Very grand. It has pride of place on my mantelpiece.'

Lucy giggled. These days, 'stiffie' didn't mean 'upmarket invitation' to her.

'Lucy, there's something I want to talk to you about,' Dorland added, suddenly looking unfamiliarly serious. 'Come here and sit down for a minute.'

'What's wrong?' Lucy asked him, as soon as they were tucked away in a corner.

'One of my snappers mentioned that he'd seen you having lunch at the Pont Street Brasserie the other week with Andrew Walker.'

Lucy could feel herself starting to colour up guiltily. What bad luck. She had seen the paparazzi outside the Brasserie, and she should have guessed she would be spotted. Dorland had eyes and ears everywhere.

'He knows my cousin,' she answered as casually as she could, but Dorland was shaking his head.

'He's a really bad guy, Lucy. Don't get involved with him.'

The shock of Dorland looking so serious and saying something so appalling made her stare at him uneasily. 'What do you mean?'

'How much do you know about him?' Dorland asked her.

'He's a very successful entrepreneur who has built up a turnkey business based in London supplying concierge services for wealthy people who don't have time to sort out their own domestic support services.'

'That's the legitimate tip of the iceberg of his business,' Dorland told her flatly. 'The truth is that he works for a group of Eastern European mafia-type thugs, fronting a money-laundering exercise. The workers he uses in his turnkey business are mostly illegals, brought into this country to work in fear for their lives. The poor sods have to pay thousands to get into this country in the first place, and then when they get here they're told that they can be sent back at any minute if the authorities find out about them. So they're forced to work for next to nothing and housed like battery chickens.

'And that isn't the worst of it. Young women—*girls*—sometimes sold by their families, sometimes just stolen, are sold into prostitution and passed from owner to owner. What he's involved in is the cruellest business in the world. He traffics in human misery and degradation. And, by the way, Andrew Walker isn't even his real name.'

'How can you know all this?' Lucy protested.

'I know because last year he approached me with an offer to buy his way into *A-List Life*. He said that he was looking for somewhere to invest the profits from his turnkey business. He talked about taking *A-List Life* into Europe and even Russia. I admit for while I was tempted, and not just because of the money he was talking about—which was phenomenal. But once I started looking a little deeper and asking questions all sorts of stuff started crawling out of the woodwork.

'The reason he wanted to buy into *A-List Life* was because he's looking for ways and means to launder the money he's making from trading in refugees and prostitutes. He told me about an idea he'd had for us to employ our own *A-List Life* girls as "hostesses" at celeb events. The way he described it, it sounded perfectly above board and respectable.' Dorland shook his head. 'It wasn't. What he meant, of course, was that he wanted to use *A-List Life* to supply upmarket prostitutes.'

With every word Dorland spoke, Lucy's heart was hammering harder.

'I'm not going to pry into your personal business affairs, Lucy, but I know how these people work—they offer of a terrific business deal made in secret and kept that way. If that's why you were having lunch with him, then take my advice and don't get involved.'

'But if he's as bad as you say, why haven't the authorities done anything about it?' Lucy asked Dorland unhappily.

'Probably because he's too clever for them to prove anything. The only reason *I* know is because I asked around— and I asked the right people. London has its share of Russian oligarchs, some of whom I happen to know, and they know people who know other people, et cetera. They aren't involved in any way with him, or what he does, but they have contacts who have contacts, and they know the people he does business with. And I was told—don't get involved. He and those he works for play very dirty. Have you told Marcus about lunching with him?'

Lucy shook her head.

'No. And I...I couldn't. Not now.'

'No. He definitely wouldn't like it,' Dorland agreed.

'We only had a meeting, that was all,' Lucy stressed. 'Nothing more.'

'Well, if I were you, Lucy, I'd make sure that there aren't any more meetings. And I'd also make sure that Walker knows you aren't interested in any proposals he may put to you, either now or at any time in the future. It's none of my business, I know that, but I've always had a bit of soft spot for Prêt a Party and for you. You've got class, Lucy, and I like that. I admire what you did with Prêt a Party, even if things haven't worked out. But it's just the kind of outfit he's looking for, and once he drags you down into the dirt with him I'm afraid you'll have the devil's own job getting out of it again. These people know how to keep their victims trapped and dependent on them, and like as not they'll drag Marcus down with you.'

Lucy looked at the letter she had just finished checking. It was to Andrew Walker, telling him that since she was shortly to get married she had decided against going ahead with the business venture they had discussed. Her husband was going to become her new business partner, she had added, untruthfully.

She signed it, then folded it carefully and put it in the envelope she had already addressed.

Just to make sure that Andrew Walker did receive it she was going to the post office with it right now, so that she could send it for guaranteed delivery.

She gave a small shudder as she sealed the envelope. Thank heavens Dorland had alerted her to the real nature of Andrew Walker's business. She just wished that the authorities could do something to prevent him from continuing with his evil trade. But when she had said as much to Dorland, Dorland had shaken his head and told her grimly, 'Removing him wouldn't solve the problem. There will be a hundred or more other men all too willing to take his place. Illegal workers are big business, and men like Walker get a double pay-off—firstly when the poor devils pay for what they believe is going to be their freedom in another country, and secondly when they have to pay over most of their wages to buy the silence of the very people responsible for them being there. They can't win, and men like Walker can't lose. And that's why it's so hard for the authorities to do anything. Their victims are too afraid to say anything.'

And Prêt a Party would have been an ideal money-laundering vehicle for them, Lucy recognised. All the more so because it was so labour-intensive, and in a way that used casual labour.

Thank goodness she hadn't told Marcus about it. He would probably have been too worldly aware to fall into the trap she had, and she could just imagine what he would have had to say about the situation if he'd known how easily she had fallen for Andrew Walker's smooth words. No doubt he would have also immediately reminded her that she had already proved her naïveté once, by marrying Nick and letting him defraud her, and that there was no need for her to compound her folly.

Marcus. He would be back later this afternoon, and then tomorrow they were driving down to the country for the christening.

Marcus. Didn't she already have enough to worry about without this added problem of Andrew Walker and the trap he had set for her?

'You're very quiet.'

'Am I?' Lucy gave Marcus a too-bright smile, glad of the glaring sunlight that meant she could hide behind her sunglasses as Marcus drove them towards the motorway, *en route* to the christening. They were going down a couple of days early so that Lucy, Carly and Julia could have some time together before the other guests arrived, and Lucy was really looking forward to seeing her two oldest friends.

Marcus had booked them into a small manorhouse hotel, teasing her that they could 'practise for their honeymoon,' which they were actually taking in the Caribbean.

She had missed him desperately while he had been away, but last night when he had returned she had felt so on edge about the Andrew Walker business, and so guilty, that she had just not been able to relax with him.

Not even in bed.

'How did the football boot do go?'

'Oh, fine.' Lucy could feel her face burning, simply because of the association between that event, Dorland's revelations and her own guilt.

Marcus frowned as he listened to her. Something had changed while he had been away. Lucy had changed, he thought grimly. Why? Because she was still having second thoughts about their marriage? His mouth hardened. He had no intentions of giving her up. Not to anyone. And if her doubts were being caused by a longing for Nick Blayne, he was most certainly not giving her up. Couldn't she see how much better off she would be with him?

'I've spoken to McVicar and told him that I intend to make a cash injection into Prêt a Party's bank account sufficient to clear any outstanding debts, and the bank overdraft, plus allow for a small amount of working capital.'

'No!'

Lucy realised that her instinctive objection had been louder than she had anticipated, but she pressed on doggedly. 'I've already told you that I don't want you to do that. I have enough left in my own trust fund to do almost all of it, Marcus.'

Marcus's mouth thinned, whilst Lucy's face burned from her anguished dread of Marcus reminding her of what a fool she had been over Nick. But how could she tell anyone, and most especially Marcus, that she had felt so guilty about marrying Nick when she didn't love him that she had felt unable to question anything he did?

'I realise that you are so rich it doesn't matter if you have to pay off my debts for me, Marcus, but I don't want

you to do that. I'd rather pay them off myself. I don't want
to feel financially indebted to you over my business.'

'Very well, then. If you feel like that, why don't I join
you in Prêt a Party as a partner? We could be—'

Sleeping partners, he had been about to say. But before
he could do so Lucy burst out sharply, 'No! No. I don't
want that.'

Why? Marcus wanted to ask her. But he could see how
upset and angry she was getting, and he was afraid... He
was afraid, Marcus acknowledged, on a sudden unfamiliar
surge of shock that gripped his belly in sharp talons and
caused a pain he had never previously experienced.

He was afraid of losing her, he recognised. Did she still
love Blayne, despite the appalling way in which her ex-
husband had treated her? Blayne had left her for another
woman, but was Lucy hoping that one day he might come
back? Did she think that by hanging on to Prêt a Party she
might one day entice him to return?

What was happening? She had seemed happy to be with
him, happy about their future—and certainly happy with
him in bed. *Had seemed*... But last night she had stood
stiffly in his arms until he had let her go, and now, today,
she was behaving though he was the last person she
wanted to be with.

On a coruscating surge of pain, he recognised that
Lucy's refusal to allow him to help was actually *hurting*
him. How could that be? Why could it be?

Lucy pressed her fingers to her aching temples. She
wished desperately that their relationship were different,
that she could confide in Marcus and tell him all about
Andrew Walker and his approach to her. But she couldn't.

'We're leaving the motorway at the next junction,' she
heard Marcus telling her after a while, adding, 'The hotel
is only a few miles further on. I thought we'd go there

first, and leave our things. What time did you say Julia and Silas are expecting us?'

'Any time after two, Jules said. So there's no immediate rush.' Would he recognise that she was trying to hint to him that she would welcome some time alone with him before they went to see Jules and Silas and the new baby? It could be an opportunity for her to make some small amends for last night, to show both him and herself that her inability to respond to him then wasn't some kind of ominous portent. Lucy hoped so. For his sake or for her own?

'It looks as though they're going to be lucky with the weather too,' she added inanely. 'The forecast is good for the whole weekend.'

'This is our exit junction,' Marcus told her.

He didn't speak much until they had travelled for several miles down pretty country lanes and through several small villages, other than to say casually, 'This is a very pretty part of the country—and convenient for London. It might be worthwhile considering it as a possibility for house-hunting. What do you think?'

'I do love it down here,' Lucy admitted. 'I used to come and stay with Jules during our school holidays, and I've always thought it was somewhere I'd like to live.'

'Here's our hotel.'

Crunchy gravel and autumn leaves, smoke from chimneys drifting like pale grey silk across a sharp blue sky, the scent of woodsmoke and fresh air: what could be more evocative of an English country house? Lucy reflected, as she stood beside the car and watched the deer in the park beyond the house as they stared back with huge soft Bambi eyes.

In the reception hall the smell of beeswax mingled with lavender and rose pot pourri. The smiling receptionist, dressed in a tweed skirt, cashmere and pearls, might have been the house's gracious owner and hostess as she explained that they had been given a suite in the barn conversion, separate from the main hotel.

'I think you'll like it. But do come over and have a look.'

As they crossed the courtyard Lucy could see where part of the original moat to the house had been turned into a pond, complete with two swans and a bevy of eager ducks.

'They've adopted us,' the receptionist explained with a smile. 'We have peacocks too, by the way, do please don't be alarmed when you hear them—some people don't care for the noise, but personally I think their beauty more than compensates for it.'

The stable block was a long two-storey building, with its own sunny entrance hall and a set of wide stairs.

'We have two suites downstairs and two upstairs. We've put you upstairs.'

Dutifully Lucy and Marcus followed her to the galleried landing and waited whilst she unlocked one of two doors with a heavy old-fashioned key.

Beyond the door lay a narrow short corridor, and beyond that an enormous bedroom with a huge bed and a proper fireplace.

'The suite has two bathrooms—one either side of the bed,' she explained, indicating the two doors. 'The sofas here in the bedroom convert into extra beds for families, and through here...' She led them to a door next to the fireplace and opened it, to show a pretty sitting-cum-breakfast room with a balcony and views over the countryside.

'Well?' Marcus asked Lucy.

'It's lovely,' she told the receptionist warmly.

'Good, I'm glad you like it. I'll get someone to help you with your luggage.'

'Marcus, this is gorgeous,' Lucy told him as soon as they were alone. 'Very romantic. Especially with the fire.' She moved towards him. She had been so on edge and filled with guilt last night, following Dorland's revelations, that she had not dared let him hold her in case she broke down and sobbed the whole thing out on his shoulder. But right now she was aching for him so much. Why didn't she just put the whole sorry episode of Andrew Walker behind her and enjoy being with Marcus instead?

'Mmm. Look, we'd better get a move on. It took us slightly longer to get here than I expected.'

Marcus was turning way from her, ignoring her subtle hint that she would like him to take her to bed. She recognised the signs easily. After all, she had experienced them often enough at Nick's hands.

CHAPTER EIGHT

'LUCY!'

Lucy forced herself to smile as Julia hugged her tightly, and grinned.

'You're here! Oh, I am so excited. And Marcus too. Let me see the ring. Oh, *Lucy*! Of course Silas insists that he always felt there were some pretty strong undercurrents going on between you and Marcus—don't you, darling?' Julia appealed to her husband.

'Well, let's just say that your sex doesn't always have an exclusive hold on intuition, does it, son?' Silas addressed the blue-wrapped bundle he was holding mock-solemnly. 'Actually it was Lucy who gave the game away, to be honest. It's so rare to see you getting wound up about anything or anyone, Lucy, that I couldn't help but wonder if there was something else going on when you kept on insisting that you hated Marcus. And, as we all know...'

'Hatred is akin to love,' Julia chimed in with Silas, and they exchanged amused looks.

Lucy could feel her face starting to burn. Hastily she reached out her arms and begged, 'Silas, please let me hold my new godson-to-be.'

'He's heavy, Lucy,' Julia warned her, suddenly all proud mother, wanting them to recognise her still tiny son's promise of adult male strength to come.

'Carly rang just before you arrived, by the way. She and Ricardo should be here soon. You know that they've rented a house in the village for the weekend?'

'Yes, she e-mailed to tell me.'

119

'I'd have liked to offer you all room here, but we've already got my family, and Silas's descending on Gramps tomorrow. Are you sure my son isn't getting too heavy for you?' she demanded. They were all standing in the large, slightly draughty drawing room Julia had taken them to, and, sensing that her friend was already eager for the return of her baby, Lucy smiled down at him, stroking his cheek gently with her finger as she walked over to Julia and handed him back.

Marcus was standing with Silas, supposedly listening to what Silas was saying about the current situation with the dollar, but he couldn't stop himself from watching her. Julia might be baby Nat's mother, but it was Lucy, with her doting, blissed-out expression, whose face was that of a traditional radiant Madonna—all soft, beatific love. There was a feeling in his heart as though it were being wrenched apart by two giant fists. Angrily he struggled to suppress it.

As she handed Nat back to Julia, Lucy couldn't help reflecting desolately that if Marcus continued to behave as coldly towards her as he had done earlier, in their hotel suite, then if she wasn't already pregnant she would probably never hold a child of her own. What was it about her that made her so undesirable and so undesired by the very men who were supposed to want her? First Nick and now Marcus. She looked over to where Marcus was standing with Silas, the two men deep in conversation.

'Lucy, come and sit down,' Julia invited, patting the empty space on the sofa next to her.

'I'm so glad about you and Marcus.' She beamed as Lucy obeyed her instruction. 'I know how unhappy Nick made you, and I've felt so guilty about that because you met him through me. Marcus will—' She broke off as a large Mercedes swept past the window, then exclaimed happily, 'Oh, good, that will be Carly and Ricardo.'

Five minutes later the large room was full of the sound of warmly excited female voices as the three women exchanged news and gossip.

'Just look at how much he's grown,' Lucy exclaimed in awe as she admired Carly and Ricardo's son before adding, 'And look at you, too, Carly—six months pregnant and yet you look as stunning and elegant as ever.'

With so much to say to one another, and two adorable babies to admire, Lucy started to relax, her earlier forced smile giving way to one that was far more natural. So much so, in fact, that when Marcus came over to where she was seated with Carly and Julia and the children, and placed a hand on her shoulder, she had to tense her whole body to stop herself from leaning into him and letting him see how much he meant to her.

'I am *so* looking forward to the wedding, Lucy,' Carly announced excitedly. 'After all, you're the only one of the three of us to have a proper regulation do.'

'Oh, yes, I'm looking forward to it, too,' Julia chimed in. 'When did you first realise you loved Lucy, Marcus?' she asked him.

Lucy immediately dipped her head, so her hair swung forward to conceal her expression.

'Not soon enough,' Marcus responded calmly. 'If I had, she would never have been allowed to marry Blayne.'

Everyone laughed, and Lucy let her pent-up breath leak away in shaky relief. What had she been afraid he might say? That he didn't love her at all? Marcus was far too cerebral to make a slip like that.

'That was a very pleasant evening.'

'I'm glad you enjoyed it,' Lucy replied as the lights of

Julia's grandfather's house were left behind them and Marcus's Bentley purred softly onto the main road.

'I'm even more convinced now, if we *are* going to think of buying a house outside London, that this would be a good area to consider. What do you think?'

'Like I said before, it is a very pretty part of the country,' Lucy agreed. 'And Julia did say that she and Silas are hoping that ultimately they will be spending more time here. Of course when Julia's grandfather dies Silas will inherit the title and the house, but they both want their children to grow up knowing their English heritage as well as their American heritage.'

She leaned back in her seat and closed her eyes. It *had* been a good evening, with the three men getting on as well as the women did themselves. There had even been whole moments when she had almost managed to persuade herself that she and Marcus were a normal soon-to-be married couple.

She certainly wished that they were. Just as she wished that right now they were going back to their hotel suite as genuine lovers who just couldn't wait to be alone together.

Lucy had fallen asleep within minutes of them leaving her friends, and as he brought the car to a halt in the hotel car park Marcus turned in his seat to look at her. He would be glad when she was safely married to him and he could once again focus his attention on the bank, instead of constantly having to be on his guard in case Lucy tried to change her mind and refuse to go through with their marriage.

He reached out and touched her arm, saying calmly, 'Lucy—wake up. We're here.'

'Marcus?' Emotion illuminated her whole face as she looked back at him. Suddenly Marcus felt as though he had been kicked in the chest and deprived of the ability to breathe. Something—a feeling—a need—roared through him, threatening to blast apart the fixed standing stones of his beliefs.

Oblivious to what was happening to him, Lucy continued sleepily, 'I was just dreaming about you and...'

'And?' Marcus probed, his voice rusty as he fought back an unfamiliar urge to take hold of her and go on holding her, so that he could satisfy his need to physically experience the reality of her.

'Nothing.' Lucy shook her head, but she could feel her face going a betraying shade of pink. It was obvious that Marcus had guessed just what she had been dreaming, too, because all of sudden there was a very definite gleam in his eyes.

'Do I take it from that pretty pink flush that it was the kind of dream I would enjoy turning into reality?' he asked, as his own body responded to the desire he could see in her eyes.

It took Lucy several speeded-up heartbeats to recognise that Marcus was actually flirting with her, and several more to take a deep breath, jettison her pride and answer him boldly. 'Well, *I* would certainly enjoy you doing so, Marcus. *Marcus*!' she protested breathlessly, as suddenly he kissed her so fiercely that she could hardly breathe.

'Come on,' he commanded, releasing her and then getting out of the car and going round to open the passenger door for her.

Their journey from the car to their suite was accomplished in between so many kisses that Lucy felt half delirious with desire by the time they reached their room. Holding her within one arm, Marcus continued to kiss her while he inserted the key in the lock and turned the handle.

A fire was burning in the hearth, the maid had been up

and closed the curtains, and the room itself smelled of pine logs and warmth and intimacy.

'Marcus...' she whispered eagerly.

'Mmm?'

'Hurry.'

'Like this, do you mean?'

He was touching her, despite the fact that they were both still fully dressed, so that her whole body convulsed.

'My clothes...' she protested, wanting to be rid of them. But her body was telling Marcus that it didn't want to wait—and, he realised fiercely, neither did his own.

He took her quickly and hotly, there and then, in the shadowy bedroom, compelled and driven by his need to possess her and make her his in a way that was totally outside anything he had ever previously experienced.

She loved what he was doing—and the way he was doing it, Lucy thought dizzily as she wrapped her legs around him and felt the swift surges of pleasure grip her. Later there would be time to undress, to pleasure one another more slowly and thoroughly, but right now this was exactly what she wanted and how she wanted it. How she wanted him.

She still couldn't fully take it in that that a few weeks from now she would actually be Marcus's wife. Lucy took a gulp of her espresso and reminded herself sternly that the reason she was here in her office was to *work*, and not to think about the many and varied pleasures of becoming Mrs Marcus Carring. Pleasures which, right now, were suppressing the doubts that had been tormenting her. It was, after all, an undeniable truth that those pleasures were *so* many and *so* varied that it was almost impossible for her not to fantasise about them. And so...

Hastily she forced herself to concentrate on what she

was supposed to be doing—namely, updating her client files and dealing with her other paperwork. The slow trickle of new business had now become a sporadic drip—little more than sympathy and family-generated events. Which was a problem, of course, so far as securing enough future income to finance her Prêt a Party debts was concerned, but not so much of a problem when she thought of the amount of time it would free up for her to get used to being married. In fact, if it wasn't for the wretched debts Nick had left her, she could have been very happy, slowly rebuilding her business on a much smaller and more containable scale.

Lucy had another gulp of her favourite caffeine fix and idly scanned the huge double-page spread of photographs from Nat's christening which, true to form, Dorland had used as his centrepiece for that week's *A-List Life*. There was one especially good photograph of her holding her new godson, with Marcus standing at her side.

Marcus. She was doing the right thing in marrying him, she told herself firmly.

There was a loud knock on her half-open office door and she swung round eagerly, hoping to see Marcus, although he had told her that he was driving to Manchester today to see a client.

'Lucy. Good, I hoped you would be here.'

Andrew Walker.

Lucy stared at her unexpected and definitely unwanted visitor in apprehensive dismay, unable to say anything more than an uncomfortable, 'Oh! Andrew. You did get my letter, didn't you?'

'Yes, Lucy. I got your letter,' he confirmed, walking past her to stand in front of the window, so that her expression was plainly revealed to him whilst he was just a fuzzy dark blur against the sunlit windows.

'I was very sorry to learn that you no longer wanted to proceed with our plans. In fact I was so disappointed that I thought I'd come and see you to see if I could find a way to persuade you to change your mind.'

Was she imagining it, or was there a subtle threat in those calmly spoken words? Lucy could feel the sharp hammer-blows of her heartbeat as it mirrored her fear.

'I explained in my letter, Andrew. I'm getting married and—'

'Yes, indeed. To Marcus Carring, I believe.'

'Yes,' Lucy acknowledged. 'Yes. And once we are married Marcus wants to become my partner in Prêt a Party.' That should convince Andrew Walker that it wasn't just her he had to contend with now, even if she was in reality fibbing to him.

'Really?'

There was something in the way Andrew Walker was looking at her that made Lucy feel afraid.

'You know, my dear, you are turning down a wonderful business opportunity here. And as for allowing your husband to be to become your partner... One never knows these days what the future of a marriage will be. Modern marriages are such very flimsy constructions at the best of times, don't you think? A sensible woman might think it a good idea to maintain her own financial independence from her husband.'

Lucy only just managed to stop herself from gasping out loud. Had Andrew Walker somehow read her mind? What he had just said echoed everything she had been saying to herself.

'My partners and I are prepared to make you a very generous offer to buy into Prêt a Party, Lucy, and I can give you my assurance that everything will be dealt with very discreetly. The cash could be paid into an overseas bank of your choice, should you want that, and no one apart from ourselves need ever know anything about the whole transaction.'

If she hadn't known the truth about him she would have been very tempted to accept what he was offering her, Lucy recognised. Because, despite the fact that Marcus physically desired her, her fear that without love their marriage could not survive would not go away. It was that fear that had prevented her from accepting Marcus's offer of finance and his suggestion that he came into the business, and that fear, too, that made her want to keep Prêt a Party under her own control and not share it with a husband.

But Andrew Walker's statement had reminded her of everything Dorland had said to her.

'No, I suppose they needn't—including those poor wretches whose lives you've ruined to get the money in the first place,' she burst out impetuously. 'I know all about why you want Prêt a Party, you know—and what you're doing.'

There was a small, tight silence and then Andrew Walker said sharply, 'Do you indeed?'

She had made another mistake, Lucy realised. And a very bad one.

How had she ever thought of Andrew Walker's face as nondescript and pleasant? Now, as he came towards her, she could see the real Andrew Walker instead of the kindly mask he had hidden behind.

Dorland had been right. This was a very bad man. Fear pooled in her stomach and her muscles tightened round it.

Exactly the same feelings of sick disbelief and fear she had experienced when she had first learned of Nick's treachery were coiling through her stomach now. And, exactly as it had been then, her first thought was that she wished desperately that Marcus were her to help her. Her second was that she was equally desperately glad that he wasn't here to witness her stupidity.

And yet she was still unable to stop herself from repeating shakily, 'I do know all about how you and your partners make your money, and why you want Prêt a Party.'

'You know, Lucy, you really shouldn't listen to gossip from jealous and unreliable sources,' Andrew Walker told her evenly. 'Why don't you take my advice and think a little bit harder about our offer, and about letting Marcus Carring become your partner? That wouldn't be a very good move, and my colleagues would certainly not be pleased were you to do that. After all, as I just said, nothing is certain in this life—especially not marriage. You've been married once already, and—'

'I won't listen to any more.' Lucy stopped him passionately. 'There isn't any point in you trying to pressure me by offering me money. I don't want it and I won't change my mind.'

'Are you sure you're doing the right thing marrying Carring, Lucy?'

His question caught her off guard.

'Yes, of course I'm sure,' she lied. 'I love him.' That much at least was the truth. 'In fact I've always loved him,' she added defiantly.

She could see that her declaration had not pleased him. He doubtless knew that he would not be able to deceive and bully Marcus the way he had tried to do her.

'I'd advise you to think very carefully about what I've just said,' he told her sharply. 'Oh, and I wouldn't tell Marcus Carring about our conversation if I were you—for your own sake and for his.' Andrew Walker ignored her attempted reply to that, and stepped past her to open the office door. 'I shall be in touch.'

He'd gone. He'd actually gone. Lucy felt sick with relief. When she attempted to stand to go and lock her office
door, to make sure he couldn't come back, her legs simply
would not support her.

She would have to close down Prêt a Party completely
now, she decided shakily. She couldn't think of any other
way to protect both herself and her business.

When Marcus questioned why she was giving up the
business she had fought so hard to keep going, she would
simply have to tell him that she had been giving the matter
a great deal of thought and that she wanted to concentrate
on them—their marriage and their future together.

Lie to him, in other words.

The sick feeling in the pit of her stomach increased.

But what other choice did she have? How could she tell
him the truth now? If she told him he would stand there
and look at her the way he had when she'd had to tell him
that Nick had not just been unfaithful to her but that he
had also defrauded the business. With angry disbelief, with
irritation and with contempt. She just did not think she
could bear that.

'It's supposed to be bad luck for you to see me in my
outfit before we get married, you know,' Lucy reproached
Marcus.

Marcus had just let them both into his house, having
picked up Lucy from her parents' home earlier.

'You aren't in your wedding outfit,' he pointed out. 'At
least, not unless you've changed your mind and you intend
to marry me wearing jeans.'

'Don't be silly. I'm not wearing the dress now, but I
was when you came round.'

'I didn't see you in it, though,' Marcus assured her, but
Lucy could see that he had his fingers crossed behind his

back, and she couldn't help but smile, albeit a little bit wanly. These last few weeks had been so stressful.

'Cheer up—it will soon be over now,' Marcus told her, as though he had somehow guessed how she felt. 'And then once we're on honeymoon you'll be able to relax.'

Lucy exhaled heavily and told him emphatically, 'I can't wait.'

There was a small potent silence during which her colour rose. She saw the way Marcus was looking at her, and then he said obliquely, 'No, I don't think I can either.'

Silently they both looked at one another.

'It's been a very long few weeks,' Lucy told him breathlessly. The look she had seen in his eyes was causing her heart to jerk about inside her chest as though he was holding it on a string.

As he stood watching her Marcus was suddenly aware of a most peculiar emotion filling him and driving him. A need—a compulsion, almost—to take Lucy in his arms and keep her there, whilst he...

He shook his head, trying to dispel the unfamiliar emotions that were gripping him. 'Why don't we...?' he began slowly, and then frowned as they were interrupted by the sound of the doorbell being rung. He went to open the door and, while Lucy watched, took a package from the waiting courier and signed for it.

'Do you want to make us both a drink while I check to see what this is?' he asked her.

She just couldn't resist the temptation to look at him, Lucy admitted to herself as she lingered to watch him as he began to open the package. When he did so, removing the contents and studying them, a couple of photographs slid free and fell onto the floor.

Automatically Lucy went to pick them up.

'No—don't touch them. Leave them.'

The harshness of his grim command instantly reminded her of the old Marcus. 'What—?' she began, and then stopped as she stared down at the floor and the photograph that was lying there face upwards.

She had heard of the expression 'her blood ran cold', but she had never until that moment imagined she might experience it as a physical sensation—as though the warmth of her blood was draining away to be replaced with something that felt like ice.

'Marcus...' Her voice a shocked, disbelieving whisper of anguish, she looked from the photograph to his unreadable face and then back to the photograph again.

On it her own face stared back at her: her mouth smiling, her eyes open, alight with excitement and delight. And the reason for that delight was...

She looked at the photograph again and her stomach heaved. Her body was naked, her arms and legs spread, held down by four sets of male hands, whilst a fifth man was positioned between her spread legs, obviously having sex with her.

Like someone in a trance, she bent down and picked up the other photograph.

'Lucy! No!'

Marcus made a lunge to stop her, but he was still holding the contents of the package. Ignoring him as though she hadn't even heard him, Lucy turned over the second photograph. This one was even worse. A woman had joined the men—a woman wearing a dildo—and she—they—she and the men—were all doing the most vile things to and with one another. And *she* was eagerly and willingly participating in it all.

She looked at what Marcus was holding. More photographs and a video. There was a picture of her on the front of the video—naked, her legs spread. The caption on it read: *Lucy Loves Lickin' Lust. Watch her in action!*

Lucy felt her stomach heave.

She ran to the bathroom and was immediately and violently sick. Shivering with disgust, she clung to the basin and turned on the taps, washing her face and then cleaning her teeth. She wanted to tear off her clothes and stand under the hottest, hardest shower she could find. She wanted to scrub at her skin and somehow remove the filth she could almost feel clinging to her.

'Lucy.'

Marcus was standing in the open doorway to the bathroom, an expression in his eyes that she distantly thought looked like pain, but which she knew must be disgust.

'It isn't me,' she told him, slowly and carefully, fixing her gaze on the far wall so that she didn't have to look at him and see in his eyes what she knew would be there. If he had looked at her before with irritation and contempt, that was nothing to how he would be looking at her now. 'I know it looks like me, but it isn't.'

Silence.

What had she expected? That he would sweep her up into his arms and tell her that he loved her? After seeing that?

'You won't want to marry me now, of course. How could you?' She was amazed at how calm and accepting she sounded. How reasoning and distanced from the wild, shrieking agony of pain and disbelief inside her.

'I'd better go home and tell everyone.' How was she managing to sound so polite? So much as though she were attending a formal tea party at her great-aunt's rather than experiencing, *enduring* what she was going through?

She certainly felt as cold as though she were at her

great-aunt's, she admitted, as her teeth started to chatter and rigours of icy cold gripped her body.

'Lucy.'

Marcus's hands felt so warm as they cupped her face, and his body was so reassuringly close, even though she hadn't even seen him cross the space between them.

'Please don't,' she begged him piteously, as her body caved in to her shock and tears welled in her eyes to roll down her face. 'Please don't make it harder for me, Marcus. I know what you must be thinking, and how you must feel.'

'Do you?' he demanded, so savagely that she flinched. 'No, I don't think you do,' he told her harshly. 'I don't think you can know how I feel knowing that *you* have been exposed to this kind of...of *filth*. That you have been dragged into it and degraded by it.'

'Marcus, I haven't. It isn't me. Please believe me. It isn't.' She couldn't hold back the words any longer, even though she knew he would not and could not possibly believe her. Not with the evidence of those horrible photographs.

She could see how darkly he was frowning at her, probably thinking she was compounding her guilt by lying about it.

'I *know* it isn't you,' he said, with an almost dismissive shrug. 'It's obvious that it couldn't possibly be you. How could it be?'

He *believed* her?

'You...you know that it isn't me?' Lucy repeated cautiously, afraid to trust in her own hearing.

'Yes, of course I know it isn't you,' Marcus replied, with familiar sharp impatience.

'But how? How can you know?' Lucy asked him shakily.

'Apart from anything else, you have a small but very identifying mole, high up on the outside of your left thigh,' Marcus told her calmly. 'And whoever posed for the body shots for this—this *abomination* doesn't.'

'Oh!'

How very weird that the most important thing in her whole life should hang on the existence of one tiny brown mole; that something not much larger than a pinhead could make the difference between happiness for the rest of her life or misery until she died—between trust and doubt, between truth and lies, between being married to Marcus and being rejected by him.

'It's obvious that someone has superimposed your face on the body of someone else.'

'But someone else without my mole,' Lucy said, as lightly as she could.

Marcus was frowning at her now.

'The mole is simply a confirmation of what I already know, Lucy,' he told her coolly. 'My own judgement is all I need to know that you could never be the woman depicted in those photographs.'

To Marcus's own disbelief he realised that he wanted to reach for her and hold her; that he wanted to tell her he would kill, breath by breath, painfully and slowly, whoever was responsible for what had happened; that he wanted to tell her that he knew not just with his intellect but also with his *heart*, with the deepest part of himself, that she would never ever indulge in the kind of scenario the photographs depicted. He wanted to tell her that he knew that she was a sensualist, a woman who loved the intimacy of one-to-one lovemaking, a woman who celebrated her womanhood in the act of sharing pleasure with just one man.

But how could he be feeling like this? He did not *feel*

things. He thought through his decisions logically and calmly. He did not 'sense' them. He did not allow his emotions to sway his judgement. And, most of all, he did not allow himself to feel his heart turning over inside his chest in a roll of raw agony because Lucy's pain was his pain. Because if he did, then that meant—

Angrily he slammed the door against the knowledge he did not want to accept.

'But why would anyone want to do such a thing?' Lucy was asking, giving him something logical to focus on and deal with. 'Never mind send those...those things to you?'

'It's probably just someone's idea of a joke,' Marcus told her, intent on refusing to analyse what was happening to him inside his head. No, not his head but his *heart*— that part of him that he had told himself, when he had finally accepted that his father had deserted them, would in future only be allowed to operate physically, never emotionally.

'A *joke*?'

'Yes, it happens all the time.' He shrugged his shoulders. 'Young idiots like your cousin Johnny, for instance, who have nothing better to do and—'

'But, Marcus, something like this isn't a joke,' Lucy protested.

'Look, let's just forget about it, shall we?' Marcus told her briskly. 'After all, we've both recognised it for what it is—at best a stupid, senseless and very tasteless joke, and at worst a malicious attempt to damage our relationship.'

'But who would do a thing like that?' Lucy asked, worry crinkling her forehead.

'Who knows? The best thing we can do now is to ignore it and to forget it,' Marcus repeated. But he knew he wasn't being entirely open with her.

He was grimly aware that only this morning he had heard that the woman Nick Blayne had left Lucy for had ended their relationship and thrown him out, and that he was now virtually penniless.

There was no note with the package, but Marcus suspected that the video and the accompanying photographs were the beginnings of a clumsy attempt to blackmail him into paying for the 'master' copies. It was the kind of thing that had Nick Blayne's grubby mark all over it, but Marcus didn't want to upset Lucy by telling her so.

Or because he was concerned that if she knew that Blayne was free again she might be tempted to go back to him?

'Marcus?'

Tears of reaction were rolling down Lucy's face. Her thoughts were a jumbled mass of fear and confusion, plus intense relief that Marcus had reacted in the way that he had. A wave of gratitude and love for him surged through her, filling her eyes with fresh tears

'It's all right, Lucy. It's all right,' Marcus told her gruffly.

'I'm not crying because I'm upset,' Lucy managed to tell him. 'I'm just crying because I'm so happy that you didn't think it was me.'

Marcus wasn't aware of moving, only of holding her in his arms whilst her whole body shuddered with reaction.

'Oh—but, Marcus, if you hadn't known about my mole...'

'Lucy, look at me.'

'My mascara's run and my nose is red,' she objected, sniffing.

'True,' Marcus agreed wryly, but his expression was warmer than she could even remember seeing it. 'But I can still recognise you, Lucy. And even if you had not had your mole I would still have known that the body in those photographs and in those situations could never have belonged to you.'

'How could you know that?'

'Because I know you,' Marcus answered her, simply and truthfully.

And it was true. He did know, at the most primitive and deepest level of his being, that Lucy could never and would never be the girl in those photographs.

And now he was beginning to know now something else as well; its message was being thumped out to him via the heavy thud of his own heartbeat.

But he still wasn't ready to give in. His desire to marry Lucy came from logic and not love. Came now? Or had originally come?

Lucy give him a small, tremulous half-smile, which wobbled slightly despite her best efforts to prevent it from doing so. 'So you still want to marry me, then?'

Marcus arched one eyebrow and told her dryly, 'Of course. It would take a far braver man than I to disappoint a mother who has planned a wedding breakfast for five hundred people.'

'I did tell her that we only wanted a quiet wedding,' Lucy assured him.

'Five hundred, five thousand, or five—frankly, my dear, I don't give a tuppenny ha'penny damn how many guests there are. All I care about is that you're there, Lucy.'

'Because you're nearly thirty-five and you want an heir?' She held her breath, hoping against hope that by some miracle he would deny her comment and declare that he loved her.

'Of course,' he agreed immediately.

Her foolish hope leaked away, leaving her starved of its comfort and filled with pain.

'I'm going to take you back to your parents' place now,' he told her.

'Marcus!' Lucy protested.

'I mean it, Lucy. You can't stay here, tonight of all nights. We both know that.'

And he knew that if he touched her he might just not be able to let her go, Marcus was forced to acknowledge.

CHAPTER NINE

LUCY had refused point blank to wear a white wedding dress, and had been on the point of giving up finding anything suitable in the short time she'd had available when she had seen a Vera Wang dress in Harrods, in ecru silk. Wonder of wonders, it had fitted her.

The long sheath-like gown had a tight-fitting corset-style bodice, a detachable skirt, and a fishtail demi-train. In order to satisfy family tradition a copy had been made of its matching close-fitting bolero-style jacket from a piece of antique family lace.

She hadn't wanted to wear a veil either, but in the end had agreed to wear a small pillbox-style hat with a very small 'almost' veil.

The promise of heavy-duty wedding-style cream lilies with appropriate greenery, a positive phalanx of pages and bridesmaids of assorted junior ranks from both their families, and the pomp and circumstance of the Oratory and Handel's music had been enough to soothe her mother's maternal angst about her not looking like a 'real' bride.

Marcus knew that she had entered the church from the excited rustle of movement that seethed along the pews behind him, and to his own astonishment felt compelled to turn and watch her as she walked down the aisle towards him.

He felt his body tighten and his heart lurch in a reaction he had been determined no woman would ever arouse in him—least of all Lucy.

* * *

It had really happened. She and Marcus really were married, Lucy realised dizzily as the Bishop intoned mellifluously, 'You may kiss the bride.'

And Marcus leaned towards her and then did just that. A cool and very distant brushing of his lips against hers that filled her eyes with painful despair and made her hand tremble within his.

Handel's musical paean of triumphal joy rang out as they walked together back down the aisle and then out into the crisp sunshine of the November afternoon, to be bombarded with rose petals by their well-wishers and guests before being swept off in a cavalcade of shiny black limousines to the imposing building built originally by a grateful nation for its hero, the Duke of Wellington, for the wedding breakfast.

'Are you sure you aren't disappointed that we didn't book into a hotel for tonight?' Marcus asked.

They were standing in his bedroom at the Wendover Square house—now *their* bedroom. It still smelled just faintly of its refurbishments—a sort of new paint, new fabric and new carpet smell, all mingled together.

'No, I'm not disappointed at all,' Lucy reassured him. 'After all, we're flying off to the Caribbean on honeymoon tomorrow, and besides...'

'Besides what?' he demanded.

Lucy shook her head. They might be married, and she might be his wife, but that didn't mean she felt she could tell him that she didn't care where they were just so long as they were together, and that anyway his house had now become inextricably linked in her emotions with the wonder of the first night she had spent there and the joy of what it had led her to.

'Nothing,' she fibbed, before admitting ruefully, 'I did

feel a bit of an idiot coming back here in the taxi still wearing my wedding dress, though. Why did you want me to keep it on?'

The look he was giving her made her whole face colour up.

'Because I want to have the pleasure of taking it off, of course. All those tiny buttons down the back have been tantalising me for hours,' Marcus told her truthfully, 'and the sooner the better, I think. Certainly before we make use of our very sensuous new *en suite* bathroom.'

'You were the one who suggested it,' she reminded him a little defensively. Her parents—very much of the old school—had shaken their heads over the waste of so much expensive London floor space on a mere bathroom.

'Mmm. I've got very fond memories of the bathroom in our suite at the hotel in Deia.'

As part of the refurbishment of Marcus's house they had expanded Marcus's already large bedroom to include a new dressing room made from one of the smaller bedrooms, plus a huge and very luxurious *en suite* bathroom which combined the best of modern, clean bathroom lines—all chrome and limestone and marble—with the sensual luxury of a large semi-sunken bath along with a separate wet room area and, of course, plenty of mirrors.

'Mrs Crabtree said that she would leave us a cold supper, and there is some champagne on ice downstairs. Don't run away while I go and get it.'

'Run away? Marcus, have you seen how narrow this skirt is? I can't *run* anywhere in it. In fact, I can barely walk.'

He wasn't gone very long—just long enough for her to glance round their bedroom and admire the clean fresh lines of its new décor.

'Here you are,' he told her, handing her a glass of the champagne he had just poured.

'I'm not sure that I should,' Lucy demurred, remembering Great-Aunt Alice's birthday party.

'I am—you most definitely should. To us,' Marcus toasted her firmly.

'To us,' Lucy whispered back, shivering with delight as Marcus leaned forward and kissed her. She could taste the champagne on his mouth, and somehow that gave an added intimacy to their kiss.

As he released her she took another sip of her champagne, and then put the glass down. She was far too excited to need any champagne-induced euphoria.

Marcus had removed his jacket and pulled off his cravat.

'When I watched you coming down the aisle to me today, Lucy, I thought I had never seen you looking more beautiful.'

'Oh, Marcus!' Lucy bit her lip, determined not to let him know that she would far rather have heard him say that he loved her.

He kissed her again, more passionately this time, and then said thickly, 'Now, exactly where do I start with this dress?'

'I'll take the jacket off first, shall I?' Lucy suggested. 'Ma wants to keep the lace and have some of it sewn on a christening robe for us, so I daren't damage it.' She blushed again as she saw the look in Marcus's eyes.

'The skirt is Velcroed to the bodice, so it might be an idea to unfasten the buttons on it first and then I can just step out of it. The bodice is a sort of corset thing as well, you see.'

She was babbling, Lucy recognised, and all because of how she felt at the thought of conceiving Marcus's child—

and she did not know yet whether or not she had already done so this month!

Marcus had moved behind her and was slowly unfastening the two dozen tiny buttons closing her skirt and train.

When he had eventually completed his task, and unhooked the skirt and train from the low-waisted corset-like bodice of her gown, she was left standing there in high heels, cream silk stockings fastened to a suspender belt that matched her gown, and a tiny pair of knickers.

'I know it all looks a bit obvious,' she told him, gesturing towards her body. 'But it wasn't my idea...'

His face, she noticed, was slightly flushed—from bending down to gather up some of the rose petals that had fallen inside her gown?

But he didn't make any response to her slightly nervous comment.

Instead he dropped down on one knee in front of her and started to kiss his way around the bare flesh at top of her stocking, pausing to slowly unclip her suspenders and then roll the fine silk down her leg, following it with the caress of his lips.

When he lifted her foot free of her shoe and then slid off her stocking, holding her foot firmly and then kissing her instep, Lucy exhaled tremulously in delirious lust.

The other stocking and her suspender belt were removed equally sensually. But Marcus hadn't finished. He slid his hands inside her knickers, pulling them down to reveal her new wax—not a summer-holiday-style Brazilian, but instead a small heart shape of silky blonde hair, something the beautician had told her was a favourite with a lot of brides.

'Mmm...pretty. Very nice,' he commented. 'But not as nice as this.' And then, while his hands held the top of her legs, his tongue probed delicately between the rose-petal-scented lips of her sex and stroked lingeringly along the whole length of her opening, right up to the now swollen and eagerly pulsing jut of flesh that was her clitoris.

Lucy moaned out aloud and buried her fingers in his hair as shuddering waves of pleasure gripped her.

'Who needs champagne when they can have nectar?' Marcus told her thickly, after his tongue had stroked her to a sweetly urgent climax.

It had still been light when they had arrived at the house, but by the time they finally made it onto the big bed it was quite definitely dark—and she was quite definitely eagerly willing to consummate their marriage. He thrust slowly and deeply into her and her muscles closed lovingly round him, her body making him its prisoner—just as he had made her love his.

'Tired?'

'Just a bit,' Lucy admitted, as they stepped out of their taxi and into the cool haven of Mustique's Sugar House Hotel.

The long flight from England in November to the warmth of the Caribbean, on top of yesterday's wedding and the long night of passion they had shared, had left her feeling slightly weary, Lucy acknowledged. Weary and disappointed—because nothing had changed—because Marcus, although a wonderfully sensual lover, did not love her.

Mustique was somewhere she had never previously visited, and she had been delighted, if somewhat surprised, that Marcus had chosen such a romantic venue for their honeymoon. A tropical darkness had already descended on the island in the short time since their plane had landed, and a handful of guests drifted through the foyer in a very relaxed manner as Marcus signed them in and waited for their room keys.

'Mrs Carring?'

'She means you,' Marcus told Lucy wryly as a smiling girl approached Lucy.

Blushing slightly, Lucy returned her smile.

'We have a complimentary gift pack of vouchers for you, for treatments at our spa facility.' As Lucy thanked her and took the envelope, the girl added, her smile deepening, 'I can recommend our couples massage, which is a massage that is given to you both at the same time in the privacy of your own room.'

'If all the girls are as pretty as she was, then no way are you going to be having a complimentary massage,' Lucy informed Marcus pithily ten minutes later, when they were alone in their suite.

'Aha—now you sound like a wife,' Marcus told her. 'Are you hungry? Would you like to eat now, or later? The hotel provides an unpacking and pressing service...'

'I'd like a shower. But more than anything else I'd love—'

'Some coffee,' Marcus finished for her. 'I'll order it for you, shall I? And perhaps we can have an exploratory walk whilst they unpack for us?'

'Mmm. Oh, Marcus, come and look at this,' Lucy exclaimed. 'It's a pillow menu. You can choose your own pillow.'

Ten minutes later they were walking hand in hand through the Great Room of the hotel. Built around an old coral warehouse and a sugar mill, the hotel had been refurbished recently to a wonderful standard of luxury.

Their own master suite in the main hotel was furnished in the style of the eighteenth century, the bed hung with voile, the furniture elegantly styled and painted a soft, rubbed off-white. A large freestanding double-ended hip-shaped bath and a private plunge pool added to the romantic luxury, and as they explored the gardens and stopped to admire the beach that lay beyond Lucy could well understand why this luxurious hotel was so very prestigious, and so loved by its guests. By the time they returned to their suite, via the privacy of the night-cloaked gardens and several impromptu stops to exchange kisses, their cases had been unpacked for them.

'Perhaps just a Room Service meal tonight?' Lucy suggested, stifling a small yawn.

'Good idea,' Marcus agreed.

'Oh, Marcus, this is brilliant...' Lucy sighed happily as she leaned back against him in their plunge pool, her body between his spread legs, her head pressed against his chest, with his arms wrapped around her and his hands cupping her naked breasts.

'Mmm, absolutely,' he agreed, nuzzling the sensitive spot just below her ear and making her shudder so hard that the water shuddered with her.

'You don't think anyone can see us, do you?' she whispered to him several seconds later, as they lay naked together in the water and Marcus teased her eagerly expectant body with all the touches he knew it loved.

'No...but we can go inside, if you want.'

'No, I like it here,' Lucy told him. 'There's something so nice about lying naked in the water and the sun.'

'Mmm, something very nice,' Marcus agreed, as he took advantage of her nudity to enjoy unlimited access to her body whilst encouraging her to do the same with his.

She had woken up this morning to Marcus stroking teasing fingers against her breast whilst feathering kisses on her closed eyelids, and they had gone from there on a slow journey of foreplay that had ended up with her abandoning herself willingly and completely to his thrusting possession. Now, scarcely a couple of hours later, her desire for him was already an urgent clamouring force.

Sliding away from him, Lucy slowly stroked her hand down over his body to embrace his erection.

Marcus watched whilst she focused on his pleasure, wondering if she knew just how much of it was attributable not to what she was doing but to the look of erotic delight in her eyes as she did so. Even her own body was registering its pleasure in what she was doing, her nipples tightening and her breasts lifting slightly. Beneath the water he could see how the lips of her sex were swelling and flushing.

'Marcus, we can't—not here,' Lucy protested as he reached for her, but it was too late, and as Marcus positioned her over the erection she had just been caressing she straddled him and sank slowly onto it, luxuriating in the erotic intensity of taking him into her, centimetre by centimetre, her slick muscles and flesh gripping and caressing him. He groaned fiercely and reached for her hips, pulling her down hard against him whilst he thrust into her, over and over again, then lifted his hand to place it over her mouth when she screamed out in wild ecstasy before sinking down on top of him in quivering release.

'I can't believe we're on our way home,' Lucy sighed, as they left the small plane which had brought them from Mustique.

'We've got a few hours yet before we pick up our connecting flight for London. Is there anything you want to do?'

Lucy shook her head. 'I'll go and get myself some magazines and a book.'

'I've got couple of calls to make, so I'll go and order you some coffee, shall I?' Marcus offered.

'Mmm—please.' Lucy thanked him.

Lucy was standing in the queue waiting to pay for her purchases when she saw him. The blood drained out of her face and she whispered, horrified, 'Nick!'

And, even though she knew he could not possibly have heard her, he turned his head and looked straight at her, abandoning the woman he was with to come over to her.

Immediately she shrank back from him, not wanting him anywhere near her.

'Well, well—if it isn't my ex-wife. Here on your own, are you?' he taunted her.

'No, actually, I'm with Marcus,' Lucy told him coldly. She badly wanted to ignore him, but he was standing right next to her now, and unless she abandoned the books she was holding and walked away she would have to stay where she was in the queue.

'Carring?'

She could see that Nick wasn't at all pleased—that in fact he looked distinctly put out.

'Yes, Marcus,' Lucy repeated. 'He and I are married now.' She couldn't resist the small happy boast.

'He *married* you?' Nick demanded sharply. 'How on earth did you persuade him to do that? Pregnant, are you? I thought he'd dump you the moment he saw the little wedding present Andrew and I sent him. Perhaps he has his own reasons for going ahead, does he? But if he thinks he'll force Andrew into paying more for Prêt a Party, then—'

'*You* sent those photographs?' Lucy cut him off, white-faced.

'Mmm...good, weren't they?' he mocked her. 'Especially that one of you smiling like you were really having a good time.'

She mustn't let him see how shocked and upset she was, Lucy decided frantically. Nor must she let him guess how frightened it made her feel to know that he was working with Andrew Walker, and that the two of them had tried to destroy her marriage before it had even begun.

She felt as though she was being subjected to a sensation not unlike the centre of gravity beneath her feet physically shifting, as though there had been a minor earth tremor. It scared her sick to recognise how far Andrew Walker was prepared to go to get Prêt a Party.

'You really should have accepted Andrew's offer, Lucy,' Nick was telling her. 'He isn't at all pleased with you, you know. He wants Prêt a Party, and believe me he will get it—one way or another.'

Several equally horrible suspicions were thrusting into her awareness like ice picks.

'How do you know Andrew Walker?' she demanded.

'What's that got to do with you? Let's just say that I do know him, and that I recommended to him that he look into investing in Prêt a Party,' Nick boasted. 'It's perfect for his needs.'

'Those needs being laundering money stolen from refugees who live in fear of him, you mean?' Lucy challenged Nick furiously.

'My, my—we have been nosey, haven't we? Be careful that nose of yours doesn't get chopped off for being stuck into places it has no right to be, Lucy. And think about this: you had already agreed verbally to a partnership with Andrew, so you are just as involved in what goes on as the rest of us.'

'No. We only discussed a partnership—and then I didn't know the truth.'

'But can you prove that?' Nick taunted her. 'I'm sure Andrew would be able to prove that you did if he felt he needed to. He means to have Prêt a Party, Lucy, and he wants it without Carring being involved in it. Andrew will get what he wants. He always does.'

She was beginning to feel sick again, and she knew she couldn't bear another minute of Nick's company. He made her feel so vulnerable and afraid. But she must not let him, she told herself.

Where was Lucy? Marcus left the coffee shop and went to look for her.

It was easy for him to pick her out from amongst the other travellers—and easy, too, for him to recognise the man standing so close to her, obviously engaged in a very intimate conversation with her.

Nick Blayne. What the hell...?

He could feel the anger sheeting though him. Lucy was his now. Marcus started to move towards them, but at that moment Lucy put down the books she was holding and started to walk away from Nick, heading for the coffee shop. When Marcus looked away from her, to where Nick Blayne had been, the other man had disappeared.

He caught up with Lucy just as she reached the coffee shop. She looked shocked and very distressed.

'What's happened?' he demanded tersely. So tersely that Lucy almost shrank from him. 'You look as though you've seen a ghost.'

Or an ex-husband.

'I'm just hot and tired, that's all.' Lucy could barely think straight, never mind speak, because of her own panic and fear. Nick knew Andrew Walker. Nick had told Andrew Walker about her and Prêt a Party. Nick and Andrew Walker were responsible for those photographs, that video. Andrew Walker had wanted to stop Marcus marrying her because he wanted Prêt a Party.

She hadn't said a word about seeing Blayne. Had he told her that he was free again? Was she wishing that she were too? Had they made arrangements to meet up somewhere—in London, for instance? They had certainly had time.

'That's our flight they've just called,' Marcus announced.

'Marcus...' Lucy desperately wanted to tell him what had happened, to appeal to him for help.

'Yes.'

She bit her lip. 'Nothing.' How could she involve him? How could she tell him what a fool she had been? How could she tell him about the seedy and immoral nature of what she had so nearly become involved in? And what if, because of her foolishness, those dark forces and everything that went with them should seep into their own lives? Into Marcus's business life? Marcus was a man of honour and probity—Marcus was the total opposite of the Andrew Walkers of this world.

She felt sick and shaky, and so very, very afraid.

'Lucy. What a naughty girl you've been, not returning my calls.'

Lucy tried to stand up, but Andrew Walker had placed a hard hand on her shoulder, pushing her back into her chair. How had he got into the office? She had locked the door. She always locked the door when she had to be here now.

He waved a key under her nose, as though he had guessed what she was thinking.

'How fortunate that Nick remembered he had a spare

key to the office here. He's back in London, by the way. Has he been in touch with you yet?'

Lucy didn't speak. She didn't trust herself to do so.

'Nick very much wants to see you,' he continued. 'In fact he has told me in confidence how much he regrets the break-up of your marriage. I must say that it is a pity he is no longer involved in Prêt a Party.'

He released her shoulder and pulled up a chair, straddling it to sit in front of her, blocking her pathway to the door—which she suspected he had probably locked anyway.

'Now, about Prêt a Party, Lucy.'

'I'm closing Prêt a Party down,' Lucy told him immediately. All she had been able to think about since their return from honeymoon had been how to solve the problem she had unwittingly brought on herself. In the end she had decided that the best way was simply to make sure that Prêt a Party no longer existed. 'You'll have to look for something else.'

'Oh, no. I'm afraid we can't allow you to do that. You see, Prêt a Party is just so perfect for our needs. It really was very foolish of Nick to give up his involvement in it, and of course he knows that himself now. Indeed, it strikes me that he may very well have a claim on re-establishing his role in Prêt a Party—after all, there was never any formal cessation of the contract between you, was there?'

'Nick left me.'

'A mistake he now regrets,' Andrew Walker told her smoothly.

'I won't be dragged into what you're doing, and I shall—'

He was shaking his head.

'Lucy, I don't think you properly understand. We want Prêt a Party, and we want you as well. After all, without you it isn't very much use to us, you know. It's your name that makes it what it is.'

'No. I won't agree—and you can't make me.'

'Oh, dear. I'm afraid I am going to have to disillusion you there. We very much *can* make you. How do you feel about your husband, Lucy? Do you love him? You wouldn't want to see him hurt, would you? And he could be hurt—very badly hurt, too—if you don't do what we want.'

'You're just saying that,' Lucy protested. 'You're just trying to frighten me and threaten me—'

'Where is Marcus at the moment, Lucy? Do you know?'

Stubbornly she refused to answer him. Andrew Walker sighed gently.

'He's in Leeds, isn't he? Why don't you telephone him? You know his mobile number, don't you?'

'He's gone to see a client,' Lucy told him stiffly. 'I don't want to disturb him.'

'He may have gone to Leeds to see a client, but unfortunately he didn't make the appointment. He's had a small...accident, you see.'

He saw her expression and laughed.

'I'm going to be very generous to you, Lucy. I'm going now, and I'm going to give you twenty-four hours to think things over. You're a sensible woman, and I'm sure you're going to realise very quickly that it's in your own interests to accept what we're offering you. See you tomorrow—same place, same time.'

Andrew Walker had gone, leaving only the smell of his aftershave behind to mingle with the scent of her own fear.

CHAPTER TEN

LUCY felt sick. She was struggling to breathe properly. Her fingers trembled so much as she reached for the telephone to ring Marcus that it took her several attempts to do so.

When the call rang out unanswered she panicked, and then tried to reassure herself that he had simply put his calls on divert. But then, shockingly, she heard a strange male voice demanding, 'Who is it?'

Automatically she checked the number she had dialled, just in case it was wrong. It wasn't.

'I want to speak to Marcus—my husband.'

'Ai want to speak to Marcus—mai 'usband.' The man mimicked her cruelly. 'Well, there ain't no Marcus 'ere.'

'But you've got his mobile! How—? Where—?'

To her dismay the line went dead—and remained dead even though she tried over and over again to get her call answered.

Marcus's mobile had obviously been stolen—but that didn't mean anything had happened to Marcus himself, she tried to reassure herself. Mobile phones went missing all the time.

Even so... Frantically she rang the bank and asked to be put through to Marcus's PA, demanding to know who exactly Marcus had been going to see and how she could get in touch with her husband.

'Have you tried his mobile?' Jerome asked her.

'Yes, but...but a stranger answered. Jerome, I think it may have been stolen, and I'm worried about Marcus.'

'Calm down.' He immediately soothed her. 'I'm sure

154

there's a perfectly reasonable explanation. I'll get in touch with the client and then I'll ring you back.'

Five minutes crawled by, agonisingly slowly, and then another five. And then Lucy couldn't bear to wait any more.

This time she dialled Jerome's number direct, only to find that his line was busy. Because he was trying to get in touch with her? Immediately Lucy hung up, and curled herself into a small tight ball of anguished fear. If anything had happened to Marcus then it was her fault. Because of her and Prêt a Party...because of her marriage to Nick...

Her telephone started to ring. She stared at it for several seconds, almost too afraid to answer it, then frantically reached for the receiver, clutching it when she heard Jerome's voice saying sharply, 'Lucy?'

'Yes, it's me. Have you spoken to Marcus?'

'Yes...'

There was a note in his voice that immediately set alarm bells ringing in her head.

'What is it? Where is he?' she demanded fiercely.

'There's been a bit of an incident, but he's all right, Lucy—'

'What do you mean? What kind of incident? Jerome, where is he?'

'Leeds General Hospital.'

'*What*? Why? What's happened to him? I'm going to see him. I—'

'Lucy, calm down. Marcus is fine. He told me to tell you that he'll be home tomorrow, as planned.'

'I want to speak to him! I want to see him...'

She could hear Jerome exhaling.

'I'm afraid that you can't, Lucy. Not right now. Marcus is in Casualty—no, it's all right, there's nothing seriously wrong with him—just a few bruises and scratches.

Although from the sound of it, it could have been much worse if the crew of a cruising police car hadn't spotted what was happening and scared off the young thugs who had set about him. However, the medics want to check him over—just to be on the safe side.'

'Jerome, please... I want to know *now* exactly what happened,' Lucy demanded, as she fought back the fear his words had caused her and tried to think and speak coherently.

'Marcus was mugged by a group of youths—Eastern Europeans, he thinks. According to the police they might be illegal immigrants, but since they weren't able to apprehend any of them they can't confirm that. They were obviously after his wallet and his mobile—both of which they took, along with his watch. And of course Marcus, being Marcus, didn't make it easy for them. Fortunately the police arrived before things got too out of hand. Marcus said explicitly that I was to tell you not to worry and that he will ring you as soon as he can. Like I said, he's in Casualty at the moment, being patched up.'

'I'm going to Leeds right now to see him,' Lucy told the PA.

'No, Lucy,' Jerome said firmly. 'Marcus anticipated that you would say that, and he told me to tell you there's no need. He'll be back tomorrow evening, as planned.'

Please let this not be happening, Lucy prayed after she had replaced the telephone receiver. Please let it all be only a horrible nightmare that isn't really happening at all.

But it was happening—and it was happening because of her. Marcus had been attacked and robbed simply because he was married to her.

She was too distraught to cry, too filled with fear for Marcus to do anything other than stay where she was, unable to so much as move, as she focused on waiting to hear his voice.

Not even the familiar dull ache that told her she had again not conceived his child could break through that anxiety.

The seconds and then the minutes ticked by—half an hour—an hour—an hour and a quarter—and then the phone rang.

Lucy snatched up the receiver. 'Marcus?'

'Yes, it's me.'

The relief of hearing his voice totally overwhelmed her. She was shaking so much with reaction she could hardly speak.

'What happened? Are you all right? I want to come to Leeds.'

'I was mugged, I'm fine, and there's no point in you coming to Leeds. I'll be back tomorrow evening.'

'Where are you? The hospital?'

'I'm in a taxi on the way to see my client. The hospital have given me a clean bill of health, and apart from a bit of bruising I'm okay. Stop worrying, Lucy. Things like this happen all the time, so let's not make an unnecessary drama out of it, shall we?'

She could hear the impatience in his voice. She tried to breathe deeply, and gulped in air on a shuddering intake of breath that almost choked her.

'Look, I've got to go,' she could hear Marcus saying. 'I'm using a temporary pay-as-you-go mobile—all I've had time to get. I'll ring you tonight.'

'Promise me that you really are all right,' Lucy demanded emotionally.

'I really am all right,' Marcus assured her calmly.

*   *   *

This time it wasn't shock with which she reacted to Andrew Walker's appearance in her office, but instead a blend of sick despair and exhaustion.

She had been awake all night, worrying and thinking, and it showed in Lucy's face as she turned to face her tormentor.

'I do hope you've given some serious thought to what I said to you yesterday, Lucy,' he told her smoothly. 'But just in case you didn't take me seriously, I've brought along a few photographs for you to look at.'

Lucy flinched as he leaned over her and laid them out neatly on her desk. They were slightly out of focus, as though they had been taken in a hurry and not by an expert, but they were still plain enough to send a shock of sick recoil hammering through her body.

Marcus being punched and then kicked as he lay on the ground surrounded by his four assailants.

Lucy only just managed not to cry out as she saw from one photograph a boot being aimed at his face, and then in another the murderous gleam of sunlight on a sharp knife.

'This time Marcus was lucky. The police arrived in time to stop him from suffering anything more than a few cuts and bruises. Next time he won't be so lucky, Lucy. And there will be a next time.'

Very deliberately he reached into his pocket and withdrew a mobile phone—Marcus's phone, Lucy realised, as a sick, sweating trembling took hold of her.

'This time all I asked for was his telephone as proof that my orders had been carried out, but next time—'

'Stop it,' Lucy implored him. 'You can't get away with this. The police will catch the men responsible...'

Andrew Walker laughed.

'No way. Those gutter vermin know exactly how to

slink away into their sewers, and they know what will happen to them if they dare to betray me. One word to the authorities and they'll be deported—if they live that long.'

Lucy shuddered. She couldn't doubt any more that his threats were real—and enforceable. She had to do something to protect Marcus, and she knew there was only one thing she could do. Tears filled her eyes. The only thing she could do was the one thing she most wanted not to have to. But she had no choice. Marcus's safety was more important to her than her own happiness.

'It's up to you, Lucy,' Andrew Walker was telling her, with horrible fake affability. 'A partnership with you and Prêt a Party and Carring remains perfectly safe...'

Lucy managed a small uncaring shrug. She had gone over and over this so many times last night. She knew exactly what she had to do to save Marcus. She could save Marcus—but she couldn't save her marriage as well. Hot tears burned her throat raw, but she refused to think about her own despair.

'You can't blackmail me through Marcus,' she told him dismissively. 'I don't want him hurt, naturally, but frankly I wish I'd never married him. I knew it was a mistake the moment I saw Nick again.'

Well, that much was true. But not in the way she was implying to Andrew Walker.

The reason she had known her marriage to Marcus was a mistake was because Nick had revealed to her the danger she had put Marcus in—and Andrew Walker was underlining that right now.

She could see Andrew Walker was frowning, and sensed that he did not believe her. Panic twisted her insides. Very well, then, she would just have to make sure that she convinced him.

'I realised when I saw Nick at the airport that it was

him I loved,' she lied. 'I've told Marcus that, and I've told him I want a separation.'

Andrew Walker still wore a frown.

'Well, this is a surprise. And one that I am sure will delight Nick...if it is true.'

'It is true. But I doubt that it will delight Nick. Why should it? He doesn't love me,' Lucy told him.

That much was true. Nick wasn't capable of loving anyone other than himself.

'Nonsense. He adores you.'

'I don't want to talk about Nick,' Lucy told him. 'Ultimately, of course, I shall divorce Marcus, but in the meantime I shall probably leave the country and go and live somewhere else.'

'Isn't that all very hasty and unnecessary?' Andrew Walker cautioned her. 'I must admit that you have surprised me—if you're telling me the truth.'

'Why should I lie?' Lucy challenged him, hoping it wasn't as obvious to him as it was to her. 'I don't love Marcus. I don't want him hurt, particularly, but I don't want to be involved in what you're planning for Prêt a Party—and nothing you do to Marcus will change that,' she told Andrew Walker shakily. 'Because I won't be.'

'Why don't you wait until you've spoken to Nick before you come to a decision about that, Lucy?'

Andrew Walker was smiling almost paternally at her now.

Speak to Nick? She'd rather die! Maybe she would even die... But Andrew Walker had already told her that they needed her name for Prêt a Party, which meant they needed her alive. But not Marcus. They didn't need Marcus to be alive. Marcus...

*   *   *

'McVicar rang me this afternoon, whilst I was on my way back from Leeds. He told me that you've been in touch with him to ask if Blayne could still be considered an employee in Prêt a Party since he did not sign a termination agreement,' Marcus announced coolly.

Were you hoping that he was *still involved, Lucy? When I saw you with him at the airport, was that a chance meeting or a planned one? Do you want him as a partner in your bed? Instead of me?*

No, that was nonsense. Okay, so after the fuss she had made over the telephone he was surprised that Lucy was behaving so distantly to him now that he was home, but he wasn't really going to let himself think he was actually disappointed by her lack of reaction to his return, was he? And he certainly wasn't going to allow himself to think that her coolness towards him hurt.

Coffee spilled from the mug Lucy was holding onto the new limestone kitchen floor. Her heart was jerking in uncomfortable, uncoordinated, irregular beats that were making her feel nauseous.

'I simply wanted to know what the situation was,' she defended herself.

'Why didn't you ask me?'

'You're my husband, not my solicitor.' She couldn't bear the sight of the bruises on Marcus's face, and was terrified of breaking down in front of him and telling him what was going on.

Mr McVicar had assured her that there was no way Nick could claim to have any ongoing involvement in Prêt a Party, but she still felt desperately afraid and worried. For herself, but most of all for Marcus.

'Has it been decided what we're doing for Christmas yet?' he asked, deliberately changing the subject.

'I spoke to my mother yesterday morning. She's spoken

to your mother, and to Beatrice, and Beatrice has suggested that we all get together.'

'Where—not in this wretched castle she wants to hire for George's birthday, I trust?'

When once she would have laughed, now Lucy could only manage the paltriest of wan smiles, Marcus noticed bitterly.

Why? Because secretly she was thinking she wanted to spend her Christmas with Blayne? The pain that thought caused him was almost beyond bearing. Where had it come from and what did it mean?

She still hadn't said a word to him about seeing Blayne, and Marcus wondered how much contact there had been between them since then.

'No.' Lucy gave him a rueful look. 'Mother is talking about us all going to Framlingdene and staying there.'

Framlingdene was the National Trust Property that had originally been the country seat of Lucy's father's family. The family had retained the right to use a suite of rooms there.

'Will there be enough room for all of us?'

'No, not really. I think it would be better if we simply stayed here in London. We normally have a big family party at Great-Aunt Alice's on Boxing Day, since she's got the space, and I imagine we could all have dinner there quite easily.'

'Well, it certainly makes more sense than driving up to Yorkshire. Lucy—is something wrong?'

His question shocked and surprised Marcus almost as much as it obviously did Lucy. Since when had he wanted to talk about emotions?

Lucy's colour came and went whilst she struggled between truth and fear—and love.

In the end, love won out.

'No, of course not. Why should there be?'

'No particular reason—other than that you don't exactly look like a glowing newly married,' Marcus heard himself saying curtly.

'Glowing newly marrieds are normally glowing because they are in love with one another,' Lucy told him lightly. 'And we aren't.'

She would have to tell him soon that she wanted to end their marriage. Soon, but not yet. Please, just let her have a little more time with him. One birthday, one Christmas...she would tell him before the New Year, she promised herself.

Lucy hesitated outside the jeweller's. It was Marcus's birthday today, and tonight they were going out for dinner with his family. She had already bought him a new silk tie, and she certainly couldn't afford to buy him one of the expensive watches displayed in the window in front her.

Besides, he would replace his stolen Rolex himself in due course. It had been insured.

Even so... There was a discreet sign in the window saying that they also sold good quality 'previous owner' watches.

She could always go in and enquire.

Half an hour later she was back on the pavement outside the shop, huddling into her coat to protect herself from the icy blast of the wind, the Rolex watch on which she had just spent virtually every penny she had in her bank account safely tucked in her handbag.

It was exactly the same model as the watch Marcus had had stolen, and she was thrilled to be able to give it to him for his birthday. Would he keep it for ever? Even after they were divorced? The pain caught her breath and held her immobile in its grip.

*   *   *

They were going for dinner at the Carlton Towers—mainly because in Marcus's opinion they served the best steak in London.

Marcus arrived home just as Lucy stepped out of the shower. By the time he had reached the bedroom she had wrapped herself in a towel and was seated on their bed, his watch carefully gift wrapped beside her.

'What's this?' he demanded as she handed it to him.

'Your birthday present.'

'I thought I had that this morning.'

'Your tie? Yes, I know. But this is something extra,' Lucy told him huskily.

She was beginning to have an effect on him that wasn't what he had planned, Marcus acknowledged as he sat down beside her and unwrapped his present.

He wasn't sure what he had been expecting. But when he removed the paper and saw the familiar Rolex box he was surprised.

'It isn't new, I'm afraid. I couldn't... But it's just like the one you lost.'

It wasn't—not quite—because the one he had lost had originally belonged to his father. But he didn't tell her that. Instead he put the watch on without a word, and then took hold of her and kissed her fiercely.

It seemed to have been such a long time since he had kissed her like this—even though in reality they had only been back from their honeymoon a fortnight. And if he had not made love to her as passionately since their return then that was very probably down to the fact that she had not encouraged him to do so. Lucy had that brief thought, and then she stopped thinking about anything as he rolled her down onto the bed beneath him and kept on kissing her.

Yearningly Lucy kissed him back. She loved him so very much…

*   *   *

'You two are late. What kept you?' Lucy's mother asked, when Lucy and Marcus hurried into the restaurant of the Carlton Towers hotel.

Automatically Lucy looked at Marcus. Thank goodness it was too dark in here for anyone else to notice the look Marcus was giving her.

'Marcus, you've got your watch back,' Beatrice announced halfway through dinner.

'Actually, no. Lucy gave me this for my birthday.'

Again he looked at her, and this time Lucy suspected that Beatrice *had* seen the gleam in his eyes, and had guessed exactly what the giving of the gift had led to, because she suddenly grinned and said quietly to Lucy, 'Aha—*now* I think I know why we weren't the last to arrive for once. I thought it was unlike my normally prompt brother to be late.'

It was gone midnight when they finally got home.

'Only another three weeks to Christmas,' Lucy said sleepily.

'Mmm. Early in the New Year would be a good time for us to start looking for that country house we've been thinking about, I suspect.'

Lucy's heart missed a beat. Early in the New Year their marriage would be as good as over, thanks to Nick and Andrew Walker.

'What's wrong?' Marcus asked her sharply.

'Nothing. What makes you think there is?'

'Oh, I don't know. Maybe the fact that the emotional temperature has just dropped by ten degrees might have something to do with it,' Marcus responded, his voice every bit as cool. 'Something's on your mind, Lucy.'

'Nothing is on my mind. I'm just tired, that's all,' she lied.

'I want to get this business of Prêt a Party's debts sorted out before the New Year,' Marcus announced. 'I think we should go and see McVicar together and—'

'No!'

'Why not?'

'I've already told you. Prêt a Party is my business and I want to keep it that way. And—and I don't want to be bullied into doing something I don't want to do!'

Marcus didn't say a word. He didn't need to. The look he gave her said it all.

Lucy wanted to plead with him to understand, but how could she do that? Dorland had not been joking when he had said to her that Andrew Walker was a bad man. People's happiness, people's lives meant nothing to him, or to those he worked for; she knew that. Ending her marriage to Marcus was the only way she had of protecting him. It was like...it was like performing an amputation to save a person's life, she told herself. But whilst Marcus would survive that amputation, and probably go on to make a perfectly happy life for himself without her in it, she knew that losing him would leave her bereft for the rest of her life.

Only a week now and it would be Christmas. All the Knightsbridge shops and of course the big stores—Harrods and Harvey Nicks—had been flaunting their Christmas finery for weeks. Lucy had done all her shopping—her cards were posted, and her presents wrapped. Mrs Crabtree had taken some extra holiday so that she could spend more time with her daughter and her grandchildren, and Lucy had been enjoying showing off her domesticity to Marcus via her cooking—even if he had turned the tables on her by cooking for her last night.

He hadn't mentioned Prêt a Party again, but there was a tension between them that hurt her—though at the same time she was clinging to every second of the time she had with him.

At least he was still making love to her—every night, in fact—with skill and passion and determination. But not, of course, with love.

The doorbell rang as she was on her way through the hall. Automatically she went to answer it, and then froze as she saw Nick standing on the steps.

She tried to close the door, but Nick pushed it open and stepped into the hall, telling her sullenly, 'What are you doing? I thought you'd be pleased to see me. Andrew said you would be when he told me to come round.'

Andrew Walker had sent him here? Why was she not surprised?

'Nick, you shouldn't have come here,' she protested. 'If Marcus saw you...'

'He isn't here, is he?'

'No, he's at work. But if he were here—'

'But he isn't,' Nick cut her off. His earlier sullenness had been replaced by the slick, facile falsity of what Nick considered to be charm and what she knew to be a shallow pretence of it.

'You know, Lucy, Andrew's right—we did rush into divorcing without giving our marriage a proper chance. I admit that I was a bit thoughtless, and selfish...'

Had Andrew Walker made him repeat those words until he had them off pat? Lucy wondered cynically. They certainly didn't ring true, and neither did they accord with the look of patronising conceit she could see in Nick's eyes as he looked at her.

'I'm not surprised you regret marrying Carring. I suppose when you compare him to me, you're bound to find him wanting—especially in bed.' He smirked. 'Bed is my speciality, after all—remember?'

Lucy longed to tell him that all she remembered of his so-called speciality was how barren and empty it had been, in every single way, but of course she could not do so.

'You were my first lover,' she told him quietly instead.

'Yeah, and I guess you took it for granted that all men would be as good as me—right? Silly little Lucy.' He shook his head mock-playfully. 'But never mind. Pretty soon you and I can start making up for lost time. In fact...' He looked towards the stairs. 'Why don't we start right now, eh? Why don't I take you upstairs and give you a very special Christmas present?'

Lucy wanted to scream at him to leave before she was physically sick. But if she caused him to think that she loved Marcus then she would be putting Marcus in very great danger—and giving Andrew Walker something to blackmail her with.

'Not here,' she demurred, trying to look regretful. 'Perhaps if I came to you...' *Never in a thousand years.*

'Came to me? How about I make you come *for* me, Lucy? And it wouldn't take long, would it? I can see in your eyes how much you want me. Come on...'

Nick was reaching for her hand and pulling her towards him. She could smell the too-strong scent of his cologne, overpoweringly unpleasant after the familiarly of Marcus's cool freshness.

'Nick—no! I was just on my way out...to meet my mother,' she fibbed.

'Andrew told me to give you a message from him,' he told her, abruptly releasing her. 'You told him that you planned to leave Carring, but you're still living here with him.'

'I can't just walk out,' Lucy protested.

'No...' Nick gave a speculative look around the hallway. 'I dare say you want to make sure you get a nice fat slice of his millions before you leave, and I don't blame you for that.'

'Yes. That's...that's exactly what I'm planning to do,' Lucy agreed untruthfully. 'And I can't meet up with Andrew at the moment, Nick. Marcus might get suspicious. In fact he's already suspicious because I won't let him become a partner in Prêt a Party.'

'Well, Andrew's getting very impatient—and so are the men he represents. Andrew said to tell you that if you don't get rid of Marcus voluntarily, then he's going to have to make arrangements to do it for you. Oh, and he said to tell you not to even think about telling Carring what's happening, because that will be as good as signing his death warrant.'

Lucy had no idea how long it was since Nick had left. And she didn't know either that her body was cramped and stiff from sitting on the stairs, her arms locked tightly around her knees as though she were trying to stanch a wound that would not stop bleeding. She did know—vaguely— that it must have gone dark outside, because the hallway was in darkness.

Dissociated thoughts and images jumbled together inside her head. The first night she and Marcus had been to bed together; the fact that this weekend they had planned to go and look for a Christmas tree—Lucy wanted a real one and, although he had grimaced, Marcus had given in and promised to take her out to get one. The espresso machine he had bought her—the thrill it had given her the first time she had woken up beside him here in this house, as his wife; the pleasure it gave her just to look at him and watch him and the pain it gave her too, as she stored every second of time she had with him with the greed that only the deprived and starving knew.

Soon now all that would be over. It had to be. Otherwise...

CHAPTER ELEVEN

'WHAT!'

'You heard me, Marcus,' Lucy repeated shakily. 'I want a divorce.'

She could see how shocked he was, how unbelieving and how white-faced with anger, even in the soft lighting of their bedroom.

'We've only been married a month.'

He couldn't believe the intensity of the pain ripping him apart.

'I know. I've counted every day of it. Every hour,' Lucy told him truthfully. 'It isn't working, Marcus. And I won't—I can't—stay in a marriage that doesn't make me happy. I'll find somewhere to live, and then we can start divorce proceedings...'

'No!'

Lucy looked up at him.

'I warned you when we married that I was making a lifetime commitment to you, Lucy, and that I expected the same commitment back from you. There won't be any divorce,' Marcus told her furiously.

He wasn't going to let her go. Not ever. She was his and he loved her.

He *loved* her? He loved Lucy?

But that wasn't possible. He had sworn years ago that he was not going to allow himself to fall in love. It was as though there was a vulnerable fault inside him, similar to those responsible for causing earthquakes, and his emotions—those emotions he had buried and denied and stubbornly refused to acknowledge could exist—were causing so much pressure within him that they simply could not be controlled.

Pain, grief, jealousy, and a determination never to let her go exploded inside him with a subterranean force that sent a mighty surge of love and need roaring through him, crashing through every barrier he had erected against them.

He loved Lucy!

His passionate refusal caused Lucy to waver between wild hope and joy—and the stark, horrifying reality of what his refusal meant. She hadn't expected this kind of reaction from him. She had expected him to tell her to pack her things and leave straight away.

'All right, don't divorce me, then,' she told him, making herself scowl and shrug, and keeping her voice cold and sharp. 'But you can't stop me leaving you, Marcus, and that is exactly what I intend to do. So far as I am concerned, our marriage is over.'

Marcus struggled to suppress an unfamiliar desire to break something—because something inside him was breaking. His heart?

He had known ever since they had come back from honeymoon that Lucy wasn't happy, and he had believed he knew why. But he had not known then what his own feelings were. He did now! Why should he let Blayne take her from him and ruin her life a second time? She was so much better off with him—even if she was too besotted with her ex-husband to see that herself. One day she would thank him for what he was doing; one day she would come to realise, as he saw with such blinding clarity himself now, that they were meant for one another. He wanted to reason with her, to plead with her, but the unfamiliarity of dealing with such intense emotions was too much for him. He could feel jealousy, burning too high and too hot. It burst out of him in a slew of bitter, angry words as he warned her savagely:

'Don't think I don't know what all this is about, Lucy. Because I do. I know exactly what's been going on behind my back.'

Marcus knew? Her heart was hammering. He couldn't, could he?

'It's Blayne, isn't it?'

He heard her give a small, betraying gasp of shocked admission.

'I saw you with him at the airport.'

Marcus had seen that? And he thought...

'That was a coincidence!'

What else could she say? Lucy wondered, as she struggled to grasp what Marcus was saying to her. Initially she had thought he meant he knew about Prêt a Party and Andrew Walker, but now she realised that Marcus thought she wanted to end their marriage because she was still in love with Nick. And wasn't it better that he should continue to think that, rather than have him become suspicious and start to ask questions she could not answer?

'A very unhappy coincidence—as I believe your common sense would tell you if only you would let it,' Marcus was continuing bitterly. 'Surely you can't have forgotten what he did to you?'

'It's different now,' Lucy told him. How true that was. 'He's changed.' And how untrue that.

'He's changed? But have you, Lucy? Are you sure you really know what you want? After all, in my bed you wanted me...'

'No!'

Yes. Yes...

'I thought I did, but I didn't. Not really.'

Yes, really—now and for ever. Only you and always you,

Marcus. This is killing me, and I can't bear it. I love you so much.

'You're lying, and what's more I intend to prove it to you.'

Marcus could hardly believe what he was saying and doing. He was a man out of control, driven mad by love.

He had reached for Lucy before she could stop him, dragging her against his body whilst his mouth took and then savaged hers in a kiss of furious male anger.

Downstairs, the Christmas tree they had bought at the weekend, and which Lucy had spent all day yesterday dressing, shimmered in the window, its lights twinkling softly with promise and hope. Upstairs, in the bedroom above it, there was no promise and no hope. Only a man and a woman locked together in an embrace devoid of both, and the savagery of Marcus's anger.

Lucy felt Marcus's hands tugging at her clothes whilst she stood motionless and numb with despair.

She heard the sound of fabric tearing as he wrenched a button from its fastening, saw the dark burn of colour staining his skin as his hands gripped the soft flesh of her bare arms.

'Have you been to bed with him since we've been married, Lucy? *Have you?'*

Please, God, let her say no.

'No.' *At least there she could be honest.*

'Not yet? But you intend to? Is that it?' Why was he torturing himself like this?

Not ever. Never. Ever again. Not with anyone if it can't be with you, my dearest, only love. 'Nick...'

'Stop it. I don't want to hear his name,' Marcus told her thickly, crushing his mouth over hers to silence the words he did not want to hear in the only way he could.

Lucy trembled—not with cold, and not with fear either,

she recognised. Even though it would have been very easy to be afraid of Marcus in this mood.

But how could she fear what she longed for so much? How could she fear what she craved so desperately? One last time. One last memory. One last sip from the chalice of bittersweet desire.

She could feel the edge of the bed behind her, she could feel, too, Marcus pushing her down against it, his removal of her remaining clothes and his own almost brutally efficient.

'I can make you want me, Lucy,' he warned her. 'And I shall do so.'

'No.'

Yes. Yes, Marcus, do it...do it now. Take me now. I want you.

He had never taken her like this before, in an angry passion that burned and seared, but she was still responding to him. Her flesh, her emotions. Her whole self was still welcoming and wanting him, ignoring his dark rage, discarding it like the shell of something sweetly craved, focusing instead on what lay within it, on what she wanted within it, taking her, transforming her, holding her in thrall to it as her body held him in thrall to her, if only for those few precious seconds out of time.

'No!' The raw denial was dragged from his lungs to burst between the sounds of their breathing, the bed moving.

What the hell was he doing? Sweat beaded Marcus's forehead as he fought against the hot tide of his own rage, pushing it back heartbeat by heartbeat, as he superimposed over his savage image of Lucy with Nick Blayne a softer, gentler image of just Lucy herself.

He must not—would not give way to his furious bitter pain.

'Yes!'

She was not going to let him go now. Not when he had brought her so close. Not when, within a heartbeat, she could take the base metal of his anger and, like some fabled alchemist, turn it into the pure gold of shared need and equally shared fulfilment. Lucy clung to him and refused to let him go, holding him with her will and her muscles, mentally and physically, as he tried to withdraw from her, moving with him, against him, on to him, slowly and rhythmically, creating a physical tune that soothed her aching need and stoked the sweet hot fires of his desire as well as her own. In this she would have her way—and she would have him. For now if not for ever, Lucy knew, as she tightened her muscles around him and drew from him the response she needed him to give.

Marcus watched Lucy, broodingly aware of how thin and fragile she looked, her face too fine-drawn and her neck so slender it looked almost too delicate to support the drooping weight of her head.

He had reiterated to her that he would not divorce her, and he had demanded from her too a commitment not to say anything about her desire to end their marriage to any members of their families over Christmas.

'Have you forgotten that there could be a child?' he had demanded harshly

'There won't be,' Lucy had told him. But she wasn't sure if that was true. They had had sex since her last period after all.

Marcus had seen the tears bleeding from her eyes then, and he had seen them there again on Christmas Eve, when they had gone to Midnight Mass with her parents and his mother.

On Christmas Day they had joined Lucy's family for

lunch, and so had his mother, Lucy's great-aunt, and his sister Beatrice and her family. Lucy had barely spoken or eaten, and Marcus had seen the surreptitious looks all the other women had given her, obviously sharing his own knowledge that she was too thin and too sad to be a happily married new bride.

The Christmas presents they had bought one another still lay beneath the tree unopened. He had declared that it was pointless for them to open them, causing Lucy to run out of the room in tears.

He wanted so desperately to keep her with him; to take her by the hand and make her look into the future; to see how happy they could be if only she would accept his love and reject Blayne.

He loved her so damn much.

Did he? Surely if he loved her, really loved her, then happiness, her desires, her tears, should matter more to him than his own?

They did, he insisted stubbornly. That was why...

That was why he was trying to force her to stay with him, was it? That was the measure of his love for her, was it?

Blayne would destroy her. He would hurt her again and again; he was just using her...

And he hadn't hurt her? He hadn't used her? He hadn't almost taken her by force physically and he wasn't now trying to do so emotionally?

Lucy looked at Marcus.

'We ought to leave. You know what Great-Aunt Alice is like.'

They were due to attend her great-aunt's traditional Boxing Day family get-together.

Lucy was wearing a soft velvet dress in a mossy green. It had lace cuffs and she was wearing a little lacy cardigan thing embroidered with pink rosebuds over it, Marcus noticed.

She looked wonderful—and heartbreakingly fragile.

'Lucy?'

He saw the apprehension in her eyes as she looked at him and he hated himself. 'I've been thinking...'

He was going to say that he wanted them to try again, that he wanted their marriage to continue, that she meant so much to him he could not give her up. Bittersweet tears filled Lucy's eyes. If only she could go to him and tell him how much those words meant...

Marcus took a deep breath. He had made up his mind and he wasn't going to falter now. He had to prove his love to himself and to Lucy by putting her needs first, by accepting that she must have free choice.

'You're right. It's pointless allowing our marriage to continue. As soon as we get into the New Year I'll instruct my solicitor to start divorce proceedings...'

Because I love you enough to let you go. Because that's what love is. It's more than a person's own feelings—it's putting the one they love first. And I do love you, my Lucy. So very, very much.

He was going to divorce her!

Lucy's stomach churned and she felt acutely sick.

But this was what she wanted.

No, not what she wanted. This was what she had to have in order to protect him.

'Lucy, you're shivering.'

'I'm cold,' she answered her mother truthfully.

'Cold? But it's lovely and warm in here. Are you all right?'

'I'm fine.'

*I'm dying inside and I will never, ever be all right again.
Marcus is leaving me—for ever.*

'Lucy!' Lucy managed to force a smile as Johnny came
swaggering over, bringing a pretty, shy-looking girl with
him.

'Meet Tia. Tia—this is my cousin, Lucy. Want some
champagne, Lucy?' he offered, showing her the bottle he
was holding.

Lucy shuddered sickly. She couldn't even drink coffee
any more, she felt so unwell, never mind champagne. And
besides, champagne reminded her of that first night she
had spent with Marcus.

'Have you heard about Andrew Walker being the mas-
termind behind some gang trafficking in immigrant workers?' Johnny asked, continuing blithely without waiting for
her to reply, 'Apparently the police have been watching
him for months, and now they've got the whole gang. They
were involved in all sorts of dodgy scams—money laundering, prostitution, extortion. I'd no idea he was involved
in that kind of thing. Dessie Arlington told me. His father's
a barrister, and he was saying that the likelihood is that
he'll probably end up spending the rest of his life in prison,
along with the rest of the gang—I say, Lucy? *Lucy!*'

It was Marcus who caught her just before she hit the
floor. Marcus too who insisted tersely that nothing was
wrong, she just hadn't been feeling very well lately. But
Lucy wasn't aware of that because she was still in a dead
faint.

When she came round, several seconds later, she was
lying on her great-aunt's parquet floor with Marcus
crouched down beside her.

'It's all right, Lucy. You fainted, that's all.'

'Marcus, I feel sick,' she managed to whisper to him.
'Please don't leave me.'

An hour later she was tucked up in one of her great-aunt's spare beds, in a large chilly bedroom, while her own mother, Marcus's mother and Beatrice all vied with one another to say excitedly that they had had their suspicions but of course hadn't wanted to say so.

Lucy lay motionless in the cold bed, trying to come to terms with what her great-aunt's doctor, summoned from his house around the corner, had just told her.

A baby. She was having Marcus's baby. Why hadn't she guessed?

'Of course I was just the same,' Lucy heard her mother pronouncing. 'Just the same with both Lucy and Piers. So I had already guessed.'

'Well, I felt sure the moment I saw Lucy at Midnight Mass,' Marcus's mother insisted, not to be outdone. 'She had that unmistakable look about her.'

Lucy closed her eyes and let the tears seep out from under her eyelids. She felt so tired, so shocked...and Johnny's comment about Andrew Walker had—

Andrew Walker!

She struggled to sit up.

'Lucy, dear, do lie down.'

'Where's Marcus?' she demanded.

'Dr Holland said that you were to have a rest and that you must eat a little more.

'A good nourishing soup is what she needs.'

'Chicken broth.'

'Oh, yes. Nanny always used to say that chicken broth cured anything.'

Miserably, Lucy closed her eyes and let sleep claim her. The next time she woke up Marcus was seated beside the bed.

'Oh, Marcus...'

More tears. It must be her hormones. Marcus was holding one of her hands with both of his own.

'Marcus, we're going to have a baby.'

'Yes, I know.'

Still more tears.

'How do you feel about it?' he asked her.

Lucy looked at him.

'I...I'm glad that I'm having your baby. How do *you* feel about it?'

'I feel that I want to take you in my arms and hold you there for ever,' he told her simply. 'I love you.'

'Marcus!' Lucy stared at him in disbelief. Surely she must be imagining she had just heard him say those words?

'You love me?' she said shakily. 'But...'

'Yes, I love you, Lucy. Even if I've been too much of a fool to recognise what was happening to me, never mind admit it. I love you so much. I want to beg you to let me show you how much. I know you'd rather be with Blayne—'

'No! Never!' Lucy interrupted emphatically. 'I still can't believe that you love me, Marcus. I knew you wanted me in bed...' Her face suddenly turned pink. 'Nick might have said that I was sexless and boring because I was a virgin, but you made me feel like a woman, Marcus.'

She looked longingly at him, and then said huskily, 'Oh, Marcus, I don't want to divorce you—and I certainly don't want to be with Nick.' She gave a small shudder. 'It gave me such a shock when I saw him at the airport. I hoped that he hadn't seen me, but then he came over and he said—' She broke off and bit her lip.

'I'm glad it's just you here with me,' she told him. 'I felt so tired when our mothers and Beatrice were here. They all said that they had guessed—but I hadn't. I thought I felt so sick all the time because...'

'Because of Andrew Walker?' Marcus prompted her.

'Oh, Marcus! I haven't told you... I haven't explained...'

'It's all right, Lucy. I know what's been going on. At least, I think I do,' he told her gently. 'I've just been having a long talk with your cousin Johnny, and he told me about how Walker asked him to introduce you to him, and how he wanted to invest in Prêt a Party.'

'Is he really going to go to prison for a long time?'

'A very long time, according to George. It seems that the authorities have known what he's been up to for a while, but they've had to wait to get enough information together to convict him and the other members of the gang.'

'George? What does he know about it? I thought he was a civil servant.'

'He is—he's a mandarin in the Home Office. That's the department responsible for granting work visas and immigration documents,' he added dryly.

Lucy gave him an old-fashioned look.

'I do know that. I'm not dumb. Marcus, I've been so scared. Andrew Walker wanted Prêt a Party so that he could use it to launder money and give work to the illegal immigrants he was bringing into the country. Nick was involved as well...' Lucy shuddered.

'Why didn't you tell me? Was it because you wanted to protect Blayne?'

Lucy shook her head. 'I don't care what happens to Nick,' she told him, bluntly and truthfully. 'I should never have married him, Marcus. I only did because...'

'Because what?'

'Because I loved you so much and you didn't want me, and I was scared that I might do something silly, like burst into your office and beg you to make love to me. I thought that if I had a husband it would make me start behaving like an adult and not like a teenager with a silly crush. And besides, I'd felt such an idiot still being a virgin, because I didn't want to do it with anyone else but you... Marcus?' she whispered shakily. 'You're crying.'

'Lucy, Lucy.' He was holding her tightly, his voice muffled against her hair as he rocked her in his arms.

'Well, you wouldn't have liked me still being a virgin,' she told him practically. 'Nick didn't. And marrying Nick didn't work at all—it just made me want you even more. And when Nick didn't want to have sex with me I was glad.'

'Lucy, why didn't you tell me about Walker?'

'It didn't seem important. Not at first. And then...then it was too late. I didn't realise what he was involved in or what was going to happen until Dorland told me—and even then I just thought that once I'd told Andrew Walker I wasn't interested in a partnership with him... But he wanted Prêt a Party, and he told me that he wasn't going to let anything or anyone stand in his way. Not even you...especially not you.

'He knew about Prêt a Party before Johnny told him, too. Nick had told him. When Nick saw me at the airport when we came back off honeymoon, he told me that Andrew Walker and he had sent that video. Oh, Marcus. I was so frightened.'

'And I saw you with Blayne and I thought...'

'I would have thought the same thing.' Lucy tried to comfort him when she saw how angry with himself he looked.

'I thought you'd decided that you wanted him and not me,' Marcus told her ruefully.

'No. Like I said, I never wanted him.'

'And you married him because of me,' Marcus couldn't stop himself from saying bleakly.

'Yes, I did,' Lucy admitted. 'And that was a dreadful thing for me to do, Marcus, because I was cheating on him just as he went on to cheat on me. I knew I could never love Nick the way I do you when I married him. I met Nick and he seemed to like me and I just thought... But it never worked, and that was my fault. Because I never loved him. I just married him because I didn't want to be a nuisance to you. And then I wanted to protect you from Andrew Walker. He told me that he'd arranged for you to be mugged in Leeds. He said that he would kill you unless I left you and let him have a partnership in Prêt a Party... Oh, don't, Marcus,' Lucy protested as she saw the shine of emotion in his eyes. 'Please don't...'

'Lucy, I'm the one who is supposed to protect you. Not the other way around. Oh, Lucy, Lucy, my sweet little love.'

'Your love?' Lucy repeated wonderingly.

'My love—my one and only and for ever love,' Marcus agreed tenderly. 'And before we go any further just let me tell you one thing. Regardless of anything else—Andrew Walker, Nick Blayne, even our baby—I love you. I know that now. And I know too that I always will love you. Nothing can ever change that, and nothing will ever change that.'

'Oh, Marcus!'

EPILOGUE

One year later.

'SO, LET me propose a toast, to my wife, Lucy, Business Woman of the Year, mother of my son—and holder of my heart,' Marcus added in a lower, deeper voice that only Lucy could hear as all around them everyone else raised their glasses and cheered.

'I would never have had the courage to set up a new business if it hadn't been for you, Marcus,' Lucy told him lovingly.

'Don't underestimate yourself, Lucy. You are an extremely talented woman. Junior Prêt a Party proves that.'

'I wonder what Andrew Walker would think if he knew how I'd used his idea,' Lucy said mischievously. 'It had never occurred to me before he suggested it to even think of franchising event hire, and yet really it was so obvious. And with a baby of my own, I could see that there was a real need for women to help one another organising children's parties and christenings, and for passing on not just their expertise but also practical things, like marquees, clothes, party costumes, everything. It just makes so much sense for mothers to gather together and share the cost of everything they need for parties and to plan them together in a group. That way every child within that group gets the party they want and every mother knows she has a team of supporters she can turn to.'

'And all for a very modest annual payment.'

'Well, it was a real brainwave of yours to ask Carly and

185

Ricardo to get involved, and Julia and Silas. With the charity funding Ricardo and Silas give us, and the young people from Ricardo's orphanages who we help to train as nursery and ancillary workers, we're not just providing parties for children but we're providing education and work as well.'

'Like I said you are a very clever woman,' Marcus repeated.

'I was certainly clever enough to fall in love with you.' Lucy agreed.

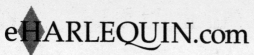

If you enjoyed what you just read,
then we've got an offer you can't resist!

Take 2 bestselling love stories FREE!

Plus get a FREE surprise gift!

Clip this page and mail it to Harlequin Reader Service®

IN U.S.A.	IN CANADA
3010 Walden Ave.	P.O. Box 609
P.O. Box 1867	Fort Erie, Ontario
Buffalo, N.Y. 14240-1867	L2A 5X3

YES! Please send me 2 free Harlequin Presents® novels and my free surprise gift. After receiving them, if I don't wish to receive anymore, I can return the shipping statement marked cancel. If I don't cancel, I will receive 6 brand-new novels every month, before they're available in stores! In the U.S.A., bill me at the bargain price of $3.80 plus 25¢ shipping & handling per book and applicable sales tax, if any*. In Canada, bill me at the bargain price of $4.47 plus 25¢ shipping & handling per book and applicable taxes**. That's the complete price and a savings of at least 10% off the cover prices—what a great deal! I understand that accepting the 2 free books and gift places me under no obligation ever to buy any books. I can always return a shipment and cancel at any time. Even if I never buy another book from Harlequin, the 2 free books and gift are mine to keep forever.

106 HDN DZ7Y
306 HDN DZ7Z

Name	(PLEASE PRINT)	
Address	Apt.#	
City	State/Prov.	Zip/Postal Code

Not valid to current Harlequin Presents® subscribers.

Want to try two free books from another series?
Call 1-800-873-8635 or visit www.morefreebooks.com.

* Terms and prices subject to change without notice. Sales tax applicable in N.Y.
** Canadian residents will be charged applicable provincial taxes and GST.
All orders subject to approval. Offer limited to one per household.
® are registered trademarks owned and used by the trademark owner and or its licensee.

PRES04R   ©2004 Harlequin Enterprises Limited

Coming Next Month

THE BEST HAS JUST GOTTEN BETTER!

#2511 THE SHEIKH'S INNOCENT BRIDE Lynne Graham
Surrender to the Sheikh
Desert prince Shahir has three rules: never sleep with a virgin; never get involved with an employee; never get married. But rules are made to be broken! Kirsten Ross is a lowly cleaner, but the sexy sheikh can't resist her...now she's pregnant with a royal baby!

#2512 BOUGHT BY THE GREEK TYCOON Jacqueline Baird
The Greek Tycoons
Greek multimillionaire Luke Devetzi will go to any lengths to get Jemma Barnes back in his bed for a night of blistering passion. He discovers her father is in financial trouble and in need of cash. Luke will provide the money—if Jemma agrees to be his wife....

#2513 AT THE ITALIAN'S COMMAND Cathy Williams
Mistress to a Millionaire
Millionaire businessman Rafael Loro is used to beautiful women who agree to his every whim—until he employs dowdy but determined Sophie Frey! Sophie drives him crazy! But once he succeeds in bedding her, his thoughts of seduction turn into a need to possess her....

#2514 THE ROYAL BABY BARGAIN Robyn Donald
By Royal Command
Prince Caelan Bagaton has found the woman who kidnapped his nephew and now he is going to exact his revenge.... For Abby Metcalfe, the only way to continue taking care of the child is to agree to Caelan's demands—and that means marriage!

#2515 VIRGIN FOR SALE Susan Stephens
Presents UnCut
Lisa Bond has overcome her past and is a successful businesswoman. Constantine Zagorakis has dragged himself out of the slums and is a billionaire. To seal a business deal, he'll show Lisa the pleasure of being with a *real* man for one week. But when the week is over they'll both pay a price they hadn't bargained on....

#2516 BACK IN HER HUSBAND'S BED Melanie Milburne
Bedded by Blackmail
By seeing Xavier Knightly, the man she divorced five years ago, Carli Gresham changes her life. Their marriage may be dead, but their desire is alive—and three months later Carli tells Xavier a shocking secret! But by wanting her to love him again, Xavier faces the biggest battle of his life....

HPCNM1205